THE ILLUSTRATED
PREMCHAND

The Oxford India Collection is a series which brings together writings of
enduring value published by OUP.

Other titles include

THE ILLUSTRATED
PREMCHAND

Selected Short Stories

To Srishti and Siddharth
bebu and mumy
bombay 2008

Translated by **David Rubin**

OXFORD
UNIVERSITY PRESS

OXFORD
UNIVERSITY PRESS

YMCA Library Building, Jai Singh Road, New Delhi 110 001

Oxford University Press is a department of the University of Oxford.
It furthers the University's objective of excellence in research, scholarship,
and education by publishing worldwide in

Oxford   New York
Auckland   Cape Town   Dar es Salaam   Hong Kong   Karachi
Kuala Lumpur   Madrid   Melbourne   Mexico City   Nairobi
New Delhi   Shanghai   Taipei   Toronto

With offices in
Argentina   Austria   Brazil   Chile   Czech Republic   France   Greece
Guatemala   Hungary   Italy   Japan   Poland   Portugal   Singapore
South Korea   Switzerland   Thailand   Turkey   Ukraine   Vietnam

Oxford is a registered trade mark of Oxford University Press
in the UK and in certain other countries.

Published in India
by Oxford University Press, New Delhi

ISBN-13: 978-0-19-568418-6
ISBN-10: 0-19-568418-4

Illustrated by Manjari Chakravarti

Typeset in Bembo 11.5/14.5 by Eleven Arts, Keshav Puram, Delhi-35
Printed in India at Thomson Press (India) Limited, New Delhi 110 020
Published by Oxford University Press
YMCA Library Building, Jai Singh Road, New Delhi 110 001

Publisher's Note

THE ILLUSTRATED PREMCHAND IS PART OF THE OXFORD India Collection which brings together writings of enduring value. The originality of his vision and his ability to dramatize universal human problems make Premchand continually relevant. This is why his work finds its way into school and college syllabi. This book aims to present the timeless appeal of Premchand's writings to young readers in an attractive contemporary format.

The twelve short stories collected here have been especially chosen and adapted for their appeal to young readers. While Premchand did write a few stories for children we have not restricted our choice to these alone but have looked at a wider corpus choosing themes and situations which will appeal to our young audience. The adaptation is minor, primarily used to remove some detail, and does not tamper with the main storyline or the flow of the translation. A Glossary has been added at the end of the volume for the uninitiated.

The illustrations, especially commissioned for the volume, are done by Shantiniketan-based artist Manjari Chakravarti. They capture the essence of individual stories and evoke an atmosphere of nostalgia for village and small town India.

The everyday simplicity—something utterly lost to our age—and the 'extra-ordinariness' of Premchand's seemingly ordinary characters have a timeless and ageless appeal. Both first-time readers and Premchand fans will, we hope, be equally enchanted.

Contents

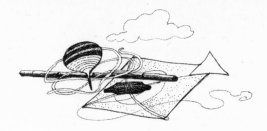

The Road to Salvation[*]

WHENEVER JHINGUR LOOKED AT HIS CANE-FIELDS A SORT of intoxication came over him. He had three *bighas* of land which would earn him an easy 600 rupees. And if God saw to it that the rates went up, then who could complain? Both his bullocks were old so he'd buy a new pair at the Batesar fair. If he could hook on to another two bighas, so much the better. Why should he worry about money? He was convinced that nobody was as good as himself—and so there was scarcely anyone in the village he hadn't quarrelled with.

One evening when he was sitting with his son in his lap, shelling peas, he saw a flock of sheep coming towards him. He said to himself, 'The sheep path doesn't come that way. Can't those sheep go along the bank? What's the idea, coming over here? They'll trample and gobble up the crop. I bet it's Buddhu the shepherd— just look at his nerve! He can see me here but he won't drive his sheep back. What good will it do me to put up with *this*? If I try to buy a ram from him he actually asks for five rupees, and everybody sells blankets for four rupees but he won't settle for less than five.'

By now the sheep were close to the cane-field. Jhingur yelled, '*Arrey*, where do you think you're taking those sheep, you?'

[*]*Mukti-Marg*

Buddhu said meekly, 'Chief, they're coming by way of the boundary embankment. If I take them back around it will mean a couple of miles extra.'

'And I'm supposed to let you trample my field to save you a detour? Why didn't you take them by way of some other boundary path? Do you think I'm some bull-skinning nobody or has your money turned your head? Turn 'em back!'

'Chief, just let them through today. If I ever come back this way again you can punish me any way you want.'

'I told you to get them out. If just one of them crosses the line you're going to be in a pack of trouble.'

'Chief,' Buddhu said, 'if even one blade of grass gets under my sheep's feet you can call me anything you want.'

Although Buddhu was still speaking meekly he had decided that it would be a loss of face to turn back. 'If I drive the flock back for a few little threats,' he thought, 'how will I graze my sheep?'

And Buddhu was a tough man too. He owned 240 sheep and he was able to get eight *annas* per night to leave them in people's fields to manure them, and he sold their milk as well and made blankets from their wool. He thought, 'Why's he getting so angry? What can he do to me? I'm not his servant.'

When the sheep got a whiff of the green leaves they became restless and they broke into the field. Beating them with his stick Buddhu tried to push them back across the boundary line but they just broke in somewhere else. In a fury Jhingur said, 'You're trying to force your way through here but I'll teach you a lesson!'

He put down his son and grabbing up his cudgel he began to whack the sheep. Not even a washerman would have beaten his donkey so cruelly. He smashed legs and backs and while they bleated Buddhu stood silent watching the destruction of his army. After this carnage among the host of sheep Jhingur said with the pride of victory, 'Now move on straight! And don't ever think about coming this way again.'

Looking at his wounded sheep, Buddhu said, 'Jhingur, you've done a dirty job. You're going to regret it.'

When Jhingur came home and told his family about the battle, they started to give him advice.

'Jhingur, you've got yourself into real trouble! You knew what to do but you acted as though you didn't. Don't you realize what a tough customer Buddhu is? Even now it's not too late—go and make peace, otherwise the whole village will come to grief along with you.'

Jhingur thought it over. He began to regret that he'd stopped Buddhu at all. If the sheep had eaten up a little of his crop it wouldn't have ruined him. Jhingur didn't enjoy the idea of going to Buddhu's house but urged on by the others he set out. It was the dead of

winter, foggy, with the darkness settling in everywhere. He had just come out of the village when suddenly he was astonished to see a fire blazing over in the direction of his cane-field. His heart started to hammer. A field had caught fire! He ran wildly, hoping it wasn't his own field, but as he got closer this deluded hope died. He'd been struck by the very misfortune he'd set out to avert. Buddhu had started the fire and was ruining the whole village because of him. As he ran it seemed to him that today his field was a lot nearer than it used to be, as though the fallow land between had ceased to exist.

When he finally reached his field the fire had assumed dreadful proportions. Jhingur began to wail. The villagers were running and ripping up stalks of millet to beat the fire. Among the men Buddhu was the most valiant fighter; with his *dhoti* tucked up around his waist he leapt into the fiery gulfs as though ready to subdue the enemy or die, and he'd emerge after many a narrow escape. In the end it was the men who triumphed, but the triumph amounted to defeat. The whole village's sugarcane crop was burned to ashes and with the cane all their hopes as well.

It was no secret who had started the fire. But no one dared say anything about it. There was no proof and what was the point of a case without any evidence? As for Jhingur, it had become difficult for him to show himself out of his house. Wherever he went he had to listen to abuse. People said right to his face, 'You were the cause of the fire! You ruined us. If you hadn't fought with Buddhu would all this have happened?'

Jhingur was even more grieved by these taunts than by the destruction of his crop, and he would stay in his house the whole day.

Jhingur thought and thought and decided that Buddhu had to be put in a situation exactly like his own. Buddhu had ruined him and he was wallowing in comfort, so Jhingur would ruin Buddhu too.

Since the day of their terrible quarrel Buddhu had ceased to come by Jhingur's. Jhingur decided to cultivate an intimacy with him; he wanted to show him he had no suspicion at all that Buddhu started the fire. One day, on the pretext of getting a blanket, he went to Buddhu, who greeted him with every courtesy and honour—for a man offers the *hookah* even to an enemy and won't let him depart without making him drink milk and syrup.

These days Jhingur was earning a living by working in a jute-wrapping mill. Usually he got several days' wages at once. Only by means of Buddhu's help could he meet his daily expenses between times. So it was that Jhingur re-established a friendly footing between them.

Spring came and the peasants were getting the fields ready for planting cane. Buddhu was doing a fine business. Everybody wanted his sheep. There were always a half dozen men at his door fawning on him, and he lorded it over everybody. He doubled the price of hiring out his sheep to manure the field; if anybody objected he'd say bluntly, 'Look, brother, I'm not shoving my sheep on you. If you don't want them, don't take them. But I can't let you have them for a *pice* less than I said.' The result was that everybody swarmed around him, despite his rudeness, just like priests after some pilgrim.

Buddhu's house also began to grow. A veranda was built in front of the door, six rooms replaced the former two. In short, the house was done over from top to bottom. Buddhu got the wood from a peasant, from another the cowdung cakes for the kiln fuel to make the tiles; somebody else gave him the bamboo and reeds for the mats. He had to pay for having the walls put up but he didn't give any cash even for this; he gave some lambs. Such is the power of Lakshmi: the whole job—and it was quite a good house, all in all—was put up for nothing. They began to prepare for a house-warming.

Jhingur was still labouring all day without getting enough to half fill his belly, while gold was raining on Buddhu's house. If Jhingur was angry, who could blame him? Nobody could put up with such injustice.

One day Jhingur went out walking in the direction of the untouchable tanners' settlement. He called for Harihar, who came out, greeting him with '*Ram Ram!*' and filled the hookah. They began to smoke. Harihar, the leader of the tanners, was a mean fellow and there wasn't a peasant who didn't tremble at the sight of him.

After smoking a bit, Jhingur said, 'No singing for the spring festival these days? We haven't heard you.'

'What festival? The belly can't take a holiday. Tell me, how are you getting on lately?'

'Getting by,' Jhingur said. 'Hard times mean a hard life. If I work all day in the mill there's a fire in my stove. But these days only Buddhu's making money. He doesn't have room to store it! He's built a new house, bought more sheep. Now there's a big fuss about his house-warming. He's sent *paan* to the headmen of all the seven villages around to invite everybody to it.'

Then Jhingur and Harihar began to whisper, plotting their course of action—the method, the time and all the steps. When Jhingur left he was strutting—he'd already overcome his enemy, there was no way for Buddhu to escape now.

On his way to work the next day he stopped by Buddhu's house. Buddhu asked him, 'Aren't you working today?'

'I'm on my way, but I came by to ask you if you wouldn't let my calf graze with your sheep. The poor thing's dying tied up to the post while I'm away all day, she doesn't get enough grass and fodder to eat.'

'Brother, I don't keep cows and buffaloes. You know the tanners, they're all killers. That Harihar killed my two cows, I don't know what he fed them. Since then I've vowed never again to keep cattle. But your's is just a calf, there'd be no profit to anyone in harming her. Bring her over whenever you want.'

Then he began to show Jhingur the arrangements for the house-warming. *Ghee*, sugar, flour and vegetables were all on hand. All they were waiting for was the Satyanarayan ceremony. Jhingur's eyes were popping.

When he came home after work the first thing he did was bring his calf to Buddhu's house. That night the ceremony was performed and a feast offered to the Brahmans. The whole night passed in lavishing hospitality on the priests. Buddhu had no opportunity to go to look after his flock of sheep.

The feasting went on until morning. Buddhu had just got up and had his breakfast when a man came and said, 'Buddhu, while you've been sitting around here, out there in your flock the calf has died. You're a fine one! The rope was still around its neck.'

When Buddhu heard this it was as though he'd been punched. Jhingur, who was there having some breakfast too, said, 'Oh God, my calf? Come on, I want to see her! But listen, I never tied her with a rope. I brought her to the flock of sheep and went back home. When did you have her tied with a rope, Buddhu?'

'God's my witness, I never touched any rope! I haven't been back to my sheep since then.'

'If you didn't, then who put the rope on her?' Jhingur said. 'You must have done it and forgotten it.'

'And it was in your flock,' one of the Brahmans said. 'People are going to say that whoever tied the rope, that heifer died because of Buddhu's negligence.'

Harihar came along just then and said, 'I saw him tying the rope around the calf's neck last night.'

'Me?' Buddhu said.

'Wasn't that you with your stick over your shoulder tying up the heifer?'

'And you're an honest fellow, I suppose!' Buddhu said. 'You saw me tying her up?'

'Why get angry with me, brother? Let's just say you didn't tie her up, if that's what you want.'

'We will have to decide about it,' one of the Brahmans said. 'A cow slaughterer should be stoned—it's no laughing matter.'

'Maharaj,' Jhingur said, 'the killing was accidental.'

'What's that got to do with it?' the Brahman said. 'It's set down that no cow is ever to be done to death in any way.'

'That's right,' Jhingur said. 'Just to tie a cow up is a fiendish act.'

'In the Scriptures it's called the greatest sin,' the Brahman said. 'Killing a cow is no less than killing a Brahman.'

'That's right,' Jhingur said. 'The cow's got a high place, that's why we respect her, isn't it? The cow is like a mother. But Maharaj, it was an accident—figure out something to get the poor fellow off.'

Buddhu stood listening while the charge of murder was brought against him like the simplest thing in the world. He had no doubt it was Jhingur's plotting, but if he said a thousand times that he hadn't put the rope on the calf nobody would pay any attention to it. They'd say he was trying to escape the penance.

The outcome was that Buddhu was charged with the death of a cow; the Brahman had got very incensed about it too and he determined the manner of compensation. The punishment consisted of three months of begging in the streets, then a pilgrimage to the seven holy places, and in addition the price for five cows and feeding 500 Brahmans. Stunned, Buddhu listened to it. He began to weep, and after that the period of begging was reduced by one month. Apart from this he received no favour. There was no one to appeal to, no one to complain to. He had to accept the punishment.

He gave up his sheep to God's care. His children were young and all by herself what could his wife do? The poor fellow would stand in one door after another hiding his face and saying, 'Even the gods are banished for cow-slaughter!' He received alms but along with them he had to listen to bitter insults. Whatever he picked up during the day he'd cook in the evening under some tree and then go to sleep right there. He did not mind the hardship, for he was used to wandering all day with his sheep and sleeping beneath trees, and his food at home hadn't been much better than this, but he was ashamed of having to beg, especially when some harridan would taunt him with, 'You've found a fine way to earn your bread!' That sort of thing hurt him profoundly but what could he do?

He came home after two months. His hair was long, and he was as weak as though he were sixty years old. During the two months many of his sheep had been stolen. When the children took them to graze the other villagers would hide one or two sheep away in a field or hut and afterwards slaughter them and eat them. The boys, poor lads, couldn't catch a single one of them, and even when they saw, how could they fight? The whole village was banded together. It was an awful dilemma. Helpless, Buddhu sent for a butcher and sold the whole flock to him for 500 rupees. He took 200 rupees and started out on his pilgrimage. The rest of the money he set aside for feeding the Brahmans.

When Buddhu left, his house was burgled twice, but by good fortune the family woke up and the money was saved.

It was *Savan*, the month of rains, with everything green. Jhingur, who had no bullocks now, had rented out his field to sharecroppers. Buddhu had been freed from his penitential obligations and along with them his delusions about wealth. Neither one of them had anything left; neither could be angry with the other—there was nothing left to be angry about.

Because the jute mill had closed down Jhingur went to work with pick and shovel in town where a very large rest house for pilgrims was being built. There were a thousand labourers on the job. Every seventh day Jhingur would take his pay home and after spending the night there go back the next morning.

Buddhu came to the same place looking for work. Once when he was going with a shallow pan on his head to get mortar Jhingur saw him. 'Ram Ram' they said to one another and Jhingur filled the pan. Buddhu picked it up. For the rest of the day they went about their work in silence.

At the end of the day Jhingur asked, 'Are you going to cook something?'

'How can I eat if I don't?' Buddhu said.

'I eat solid food only once a day,' Jhingur said. 'I get by just drinking water with ground meal in it in the evenings. Why fuss?'

'Pick up some of those sticks lying around,' Buddhu said. 'I brought some flour from home. I had it ground there—it costs a lot here in town. I'll knead it on the flat side of this rock. Since you won't eat food I cook I'll get it ready and you cook it.'

'But there's no frying pan.'

'There are lots of frying pans,' Buddhu said. 'I'll scour out one of these mortar trays.'

The fire was lit, the flour kneaded. Jhingur cooked the *chapatties*, Buddhu brought the water. They both ate the bread with salt and red pepper. Then they filled the bowl of the hookah. They both lay down on the stony ground and smoked.

Buddhu said, 'I was the one who set fire to your cane-field.'

Jhingur said light-heartedly, 'I know.'

After a little while he said, 'I tied up the heifer and Harihar fed it something.'

In the same light-hearted tone Buddhu said, 'I know.'

Then the two of them went to sleep.

January Night*

HALKU CAME IN AND SAID TO HIS WIFE, 'THE LANDLORD'S come! Get the rupees you set aside, I'll give him the money.'

Munni had been sweeping. She turned around and said, 'But there's only three rupees. If you give them to him where's the blanket going to come from? How are you going to get through these January nights in the fields? Tell him we'll pay him after the harvest, not right now.'

For a moment Halku stood hesitating. January was on top of them. Without a blanket he couldn't possibly sleep in the fields at night. But the landlord wouldn't be put off, he'd threaten and insult him. Trying to coax her Halku said, 'Come on, give it to me. I'll figure out some other plan.'

Munni was angry. She said, 'You've already tried "Some other plan". You just tell me what other plan can be found. Is somebody going to give you a blanket? What I say is, give up this tenant farming! The work's killing you, whatever you harvest goes to pay up the arrears. Were we born just to keep paying off debts? Earn some money for your own belly, give up that kind of farming. I won't give you the money, I won't!'

*Pus Ki Raat

Sadly Halku said, 'Then I'll have to put up with his abuse.' Losing her temper, Munni said, 'Why should he abuse you—is this his kingdom?'

But as she said it her brows relaxed from the frown. The bitter truth in Halku's words came charging at her like a wild beast. She went to the niche in the wall, took out the rupees and handed them over to Halku.

Halku took the money and went outside looking as though he were tearing his heart out and giving it away. He'd saved the rupees from his work, pice by pice, for his blanket. Today he was going to throw it away. With every step his head sank lower under the burden of his poverty.

A dark January night. In the sky even the stars seemed to be shivering. At the edge of his field, underneath a shelter of cane leaves, Halku lay on a bamboo cot wrapped up in his old burlap shawl, shivering. Underneath the cot his friend, Jabra the dog, was whimpering with his muzzle pressed into his belly. Neither one of them was able to sleep.

Halku curled up drawing his knees close against his chin and said, 'Cold, Jabra? Didn't I tell you, in the house you could lie in the paddy straw? So why did you come out here? Now you'll have to bear the cold, there's nothing I can do. You thought I was coming out here to eat *puris* and sweets and you came running on ahead of me. Now you can moan all you want.'

Jabra wagged his tail without getting up.

Halku reached out his hand and patted Jabra's cold back.

He got up, took some embers from the pit and filled his pipe. Jabra got up too.

Smoking, Halku said, 'If you smoke the cold's just as bad, but at least you feel a little better.'

Jabra looked at him with eyes overflowing with love.

'You have to put up with just one more cold night. Tomorrow I'll spread some straw. When you bed down in that you won't feel the cold.'

Jabra put his paws on Halku's knees and brought his muzzle close.
Halku felt his warm breath.

After he finished smoking Halku lay down and made up his mind that
however things were he would sleep now. But in only one minute his heart
began to pound. He turned from side to side,
but like some kind of witch the cold weather continued to torment him.

When he could no longer bear it he gently picked Jabra up and, patting his head,
got him to fall asleep in his lap. The dog's body gave off some kind of stink but
Halku, hugging him tight, experienced a happiness he hadn't felt for months.
Jabra probably thought he was in heaven, and in Halku's innocent heart there was
no resentment of his smell. He embraced him with the very same affection he
would have felt for a brother or a friend.

Suddenly Jabra picked up the noise of some animal. This special intimacy had produced a new alertness in him that disdained the onslaught of the wind. Springing up, he ran out of the shelter and began to bark. Halku whistled and called him several times. But Jabra would not come back to him. He went on barking while he ran around through the furrows of the field. He would come back for a moment, then dash off again at once.

Another hour passed. The night fanned up the cold with the wind. Halku sat up and bringing both knees tight against his chest hid his face between them, but the cold was just as biting. It seemed as though all his blood had frozen, that ice rather than blood filled his veins. He leaned back to look at the skies. How much of the night was still left!

Only a stone's throw from Halku's field there was a mango grove. Halku thought, 'If I go and get a pile of leaves I can make a fire of them and keep warm. If anybody sees me gathering the leaves in the dead of night they'll think it's a ghost. Of course there's a chance some animal's hidden in my field waiting, but I can't stand sitting here any longer.'

He ripped up some stalks from a nearby field, made a broom out of them and picking up a lighted cowdung cake went toward the grove. Jabra watched him coming and ran to him wagging his tail.

Halku said, 'I couldn't stand it any more, Jabra. Come along, let's go into the orchard and gather leaves to warm up with. When we're toasted we'll come back and sleep. The night's still far from over.'

Jabra barked his agreement and trotted on toward the orchard.

Suddenly a gust carried the scent of henna blossoms to him. 'Where's that sweet smell coming from, Jabra?'

Jabra had found a bone lying somewhere and he was chewing on it. Halku set his fire down on the ground and began to gather the leaves. In a little while he had a great heap. His hands were frozen, his bare feet numb.

In a little while the fire was burning merrily. The flames leapt upward licking at the overhanging branches. In the flickering light the immense trees of the grove looked as though they were carrying the vast darkness on their heads. In the blissful sea of darkness the firelight seemed to pitch and toss like a boat.

Halku sat before the fire and let it warm him. After a while he took off his shawl and tucked it behind him, then he spread out both feet as though challenging the cold to do its worst. Victorious over the immense power of the winter, he could not repress his pride in his triumph.

He said to Jabra, 'Well, Jabra, you're not cold now, are you?'

Jabra barked as though to say, 'How could I feel cold now?'

The leaves were all burned up. Darkness covered the orchard again. Under the ashes a few embers smouldered.

Halku wrapped himself up in his shawl again and sat by the warm ashes humming a tune. The fire had warmed him through but as the cold began to spread he felt drowsy.

Jabra gave a loud bark and ran toward the field.
Halku realized that this meant a pack of wild animals had probably broken into the field. They might be nilgai. He distinctly heard the noise of their moving around. Then it seemed to him they must be grazing; he began to hear the sound of nibbling.

He thought, 'No, with Jabra around no animal can get into the field, he'd rip it to shreds. I must have been mistaken. Now there's no sound at all. How could I have been mistaken?'

He shouted, 'Jabra! Jabra!'

Jabra went on barking and did not come to him.

Then again there was the sound of munching and crunching in the field. He could not have been mistaken this time. It really hurt to think about getting up from where he was. It was so comfortable there that it seemed intolerable to go to the field in this cold and chase after animals. He didn't stir.

He shouted at the top of his lungs, 'Hillo! Hillo! Hillo!'

Jabra started barking again. There were animals eating his field just when the crop was ready. What a fine crop it was! And these cursed animals were destroying it. With a firm resolve he got up and took a few steps. But suddenly a blast of wind pierced him with a sting like a scorpion's so that he went back and sat again by the extinguished fire and stirred up the ashes to warm his chilled body. Jabra was barking his lungs out, the nilgai were devastating his field and Halku went on sitting peacefully near the warm ashes. His drowsiness held him motionless as though with ropes. Wrapped in his shawl he fell asleep on the warmed ground near the ashes.

When he woke in the morning the sun was high and Munni was saying, 'Do you think you're going to sleep all day? You came out here and had a fine time while the whole field was being flattened!'

Halku got up and said, 'Then you've just come from the field?'

'Yes, it's all ruined. And you could sleep like that! Why did you bother to put up the shelter anyway?'

Halku sought an excuse. 'I nearly died and just managed to get through the night and you worry about your crop. I had such a pain in my belly I can't describe it.'

Then the two of them walked to the edge of their land. He looked: the whole field had been trampled and Jabra was stretched out underneath the shelter as though he were dead.

They continued to stare at the ruined field. Munni's face was shadowed with grief but Halku was content.

Munni said, 'Now you'll have to hire yourself out to earn some money to pay off the rent and taxes.'

With a contented smile Halku said, 'But I won't have to sleep nights out here in the cold.'

A Catastrophe*

IN BANARAS DISTRICT THERE IS A VILLAGE CALLED BIRA IN
which an old, childless widow used to live. She was a
Gond woman named Bhungi and she didn't own
either a scrap of land or a house to live in. Her only
source of livelihood was a parching oven. The village folk customarily
have one meal a day of parched grains, so there was always a crowd
around Bhungi's oven. Whatever grain she was paid for parching she
would grind or fry and eat it. She slept in a corner of the same
little shack that sheltered the oven. As soon as it was light she'd get
up and go out to gather dry leaves from all around to make her fire.
She would stack the leaves right next to the oven, and after twelve,
light the fire. But on the days when she had to parch grain for Pandit
Udaybhan Pandey, the owner of the village, she went to bed hungry.
She was obliged to work without pay for Pandit Udaybhan Pandey.
She also had to fetch water for his house. And, for this reason, from
time to time the oven was not lit. She lived in the Pandit's village,
therefore he had full authority to make her do any sort of odd job.
In his opinion if she received food for working from him, how
could it be considered as work done without pay? He was doing
her a favour, in fact, by letting her live in the village at all.

It was spring, a day on which the fresh grain was fried and eaten and
given as a gift. No fire was lit in the houses. Bhungi's oven was being

*Vidhuvans

put to good use today. There was a crowd worthy of a village fair around her. She had scarcely opportunity to draw a breath. Because of the customer's impatience, squabbles kept breaking out. Then two servants arrived, each carrying a heaped basket of grain from Pandit Udaybhan with the order to parch it right away. When Bhungi saw the two baskets she was alarmed. It was already after twelve and even by sunset, she would not have time to parch so much grain. Now she would have to stay at the oven parching until after dark for no payment. In despair she took the two baskets.

One of the flunkeys said menacingly, 'Don't waste any time or you'll be sorry.'

With this command the servants went away and Bhungi began to parch the grain. It's no laughing matter to parch a whole *maund* of grain. She had to keep stopping from the parching in order to keep the oven fire going. So by sundown not even half the work was done. She was afraid Panditji's men would be coming. She began to move her hands all the more frantically.

Soon the servants returned and said, 'Well, is the grain parched?'

Feeling bold, Bhungi said, 'Can't you see? I'm parching it now.'

'The whole day's gone and you haven't finished any more grain than this? Have you been roasting it or spoiling it? This is completely uncooked! How's it going to be used for food? It's the ruin of us! You'll see what Panditji does to you for this.'

The result was that that night the oven was dug up and Bhungi was left without a means of livelihood.

Bhungi now had no means of support. The villagers suffered a good deal too from the destruction of the oven. In many houses even at noon, cooked cereal was no longer available. People went to Panditji and asked him to give the order for the old woman's oven to be rebuilt and the fire once more lighted, but he paid no attention to them. He could not suffer a loss of face. A few people who wished her well urged her to move to another village. But her heart would not accept this suggestion. She had spent her fifty miserable years in

this village and she loved every leaf on every tree. Here she had known the sorrows and pleasures of life; she could not give it up now in the last days. The very idea of moving distressed her. Sorrow in this village was preferable to happiness in another.

A month went by. Very early one morning Pandit Udaybhan, taking his little band of servants with him, went out to collect his rents. Now when he looked toward the old woman's oven he fell into a violent rage: it was being made again. Bhungi was energetically rebuilding it with balls of clay. Most likely she'd spent the night at this work and wanted to finish it before the sun was high. She knew that she was going against the Pandit's wishes, but she hoped that he had forgotten his anger by then. But alas, the poor creature had gown old without growing wise.

Suddenly Panditji shouted, 'By whose order?'

Bewildered, Bhungi saw that he was standing before her.

He demanded once again, 'By whose order are you building it?'

In a fright she said, 'Everybody said I should build it and so I'm building it.'

'I'll have it smashed again.' With this he kicked the oven. The wet clay collapsed in a heap. He kicked at the trough again but she ran in front of it and took the kick in her side. Rubbing her ribs she said, '*Maharaj*, you're not afraid of anybody but you ought to fear God. What good does it do you to ruin me like this? Do you think gold is going to grow out of this small piece of land? For your own good, I'm telling you, don't torment poor people, don't be the death of me.'

'You're not going to build any oven here again.'

'If I don't how am I going to be able to eat?'

'I'm not responsible for your belly.'

'But if I do nothing except chores for you where will I go for food?'

'If you're going to stay in the village you'll have to do my chores.'

'I'll do them when I've built my oven. I can't do your work just for the sake of staying in the village.'

'Then don't, just get out of the village.'

'How can I? I've grown old in this hut. My in-laws and their grandparents lived in this same hut. Except for Yama, king of death, nobody's going to force me out of it now.'

'Excellent, now you're quoting Scripture!' Pandit Udaybhan said. 'If you'd worked hard I might have let you stay, but after this I won't rest until I've had you thrown out.' To his attendants he said, 'Go get a pile of leaves right away and set fire to the whole thing; we'll show her how to make an oven.'

In a moment there was a tremendous racket. The flames leapt towards the sky, the blaze spread wildly in all directions. All the villagers came clustering around this mountain of fire. Hopelessly, Bhungi stood by her oven watching the conflagration. Suddenly, with a violent dash, she hurled herself into the flames. They came running from everywhere but no one had the courage to go into the mouth of the blaze. In a matter of seconds her withered body was completely consumed.

At that moment the wind rose with a gust. The liberated flames began to race toward the east. There were some peasants' huts near the oven which were engulfed by the fierce flames. Fed in this way, the blaze spread even further. Panditji's barn was in its path and it pounced upon it. By now the whole village was in a panic. They began to band together to put out the fire but the sprinkle of water acted like oil on it and the flames kept mounting higher. Pandit Udaybhan's splendid mansion was swallowed up; while he watched, it tossed like a ship amid wild waves and disappeared in the sea of fire. The sound of lamentation that broke out amidst the ashes was even more pitiful than Bhungi's grievous cries.

Penalty*

MUNSHI KHAIRAT ALI KHAN WAS THE INSPECTOR OF Sanitation and hundreds of sweeper women depended on him. He was good-hearted and well thought of—not the sort who cut their pay, scolded them or fined them. But he went on regularly rebuking and punishing Alarakkhi. She was not a shirker, nor saucy or slovenly; she was also not at all bad-looking. During these chilly days she would be out with her broom before it was light and go on assiduously sweeping the road until nine. But all the same, she would be penalized. Huseni, her husband, would help her with the work too when he found the chance, but it was in Alarakkhi's fate that she was going to be fined. For others pay-day was an occasion to celebrate, for Alarakkhi it was a time to weep. On that day it was as though her heart had broken. Who could tell how much would be deducted? Like students awaiting the results of their examinations, over and over again she would speculate on the amount of the deduction.

Whenever she got so tired that she'd sit down a moment to catch her breath, precisely then the Inspector would arrive riding in his *ekka*. No matter how much she'd say, 'Please, Excellency, I'll go back to work again,' he would jot her name down in his book without listening. A few days later the very same thing would happen again. If she bought a few cents worth of candy from the sweets-vendor

*Jurmana

and started to eat it, just at that moment the Inspector would drop on her from the devil knew where and once more write her name down in his book. Where could he have been hiding? The minute she began to rest the least bit he was upon her like an evil spirit. If he wrote her name down on only two days, how much would the penalty be then? God knew. More than eight *annas*? If only it weren't a whole rupee! With her head bowed she'd go to collect her pay and find even more deducted than she'd estimated. Taking her money with trembling hands she'd go home, her eyes full of tears. There was no one to turn to, no one who'd listen.

Today was pay-day again. The past month her unweaned daughter had suffered from coughing and fever. The weather had been exceptionally cold. Partly because of the cold, partly because of the little girl's crying she was kept awake the whole night. Several times she'd come to work late. Khan Sahib had noted down her name, and this time she would be fined half her pay. It was impossible to say how much might be deducted. Early in the morning she picked up the baby, took her broom and went to the street. But the naughty creature wouldn't let herself be put down. Time after time Alarakkhi would threaten her with the arrival of the Inspector. 'He's on his way and he'll beat me and as for you, he'll cut off your nose and ears!' The child was willing to sacrifice her nose and ears but not to be put down. At last, when Alarakkhi had failed to get rid of her with threats and coaxing alike, she set her down and left her crying and wailing while she started to sweep. But the little wretch wouldn't sit in one place to cry her heart out; she crawled after her mother time and time again, caught her sari, clung to her legs, then wallowed around on the ground and a moment later sat up to start crying again.

'Shut up!' Alarakkhi said, brandishing the broom. 'If you don't, I'll hit you with the broom and that'll be the end of you. That bastard of an Inspector's going to show up at any moment.'

She had hardly got the words out of her mouth when Inspector Khairat Ali Khan dismounted from his bicycle directly in front of her. She turned pale, her heart began to thump. 'Oh God, may my head fall off if he heard me! Right in front of me and I didn't see him. Who could tell he'd come on his bicycle today? He's always

come in his ekka.' The blood froze in her veins, she stood holding the broom as though paralyzed.

Angrily the Inspector said, 'Why do you drag the kid after you to work? Why didn't you leave it at home?'

'She's sick, Excellency,' Alarakkhi said timidly. 'Who's at home to leave her with?'

'What's the matter with her?'

'She has a fever, *Huzoor.*'

'And you make her cry by leaving her? Don't you care if she lives?'

'How can I do my work if I carry her?'

'Why don't you ask for leave?'

'If my pay is cut, Huzoor, what will we have to live on?'

'Pick her up and take her home. When Huseni comes back send him here to finish the sweeping.'

She picked up the baby and was about to go when he asked, 'Why were you abusing me?'

Alarakkhi felt all her breath knocked out of her. If you'd cut her there wouldn't have been any blood. Trembling she said, 'No, Huzoor, may my head fall off if I was abusing you.'

And she burst into tears.

In the evening Huseni and Alarakkhi went to collect her pay. She was very downcast.

'Why so sad?' Huseni tried to console her. 'The pay's going to be cut, so let them cut it. I swear on your life from now on I won't touch another drop of booze or toddy.'

'I'm afraid I'm fired. Damn my tongue! How could I....'

'If you're fired, then you're fired, but let Allah be merciful to him. Why go on crying about it?'

'You've made me come for nothing. Everyone of those women will laugh at me.'

'If he's fired you, won't we ask on what grounds? And who heard you abuse him? Can there be so much injustice that he can fire anyone he pleases? If I'm not heard I'll complain to the *panchayat*, I'll beat my head on the headman's gate—'

'If our people stuck together like that would Khan Sahib ever dare fine us so much?'

'No matter how serious the sickness there's a medicine for it, silly.'

But Alarakkhi was not set at rest. Dejection covered her face like a cloud. When the Inspector heard her abuse him why didn't he even scold her? Why didn't he fire her on the spot? She wasn't able to work it out, he actually seemed kind. She couldn't manage to understand this mystery. She was afraid. He had decided to fire her— that must have been why he was so nice. She'd heard that a man about to be hanged is given a fine last meal, they have to give him anything he wants—so surely the Inspector was going to dismiss her.

They reached the municipal office building. The pay began to be distributed. The sweeper women were first. Whoever's name was called would go running and taking her money call down undeserved blessings on the Inspector and go away. Alarakkhi's name was always called after Champa's. Today she was passed over. After Champa, Jahuran's name was called, and she always followed Alarakkhi.

In despair she looked at Huseni. The women were watching her and beginning to whisper.

One after another the names were called and Alarakkhi went on looking at the trees across the way.

Suddenly startled, she heard her name. Slowly she stood up and walked ahead with the slow tread of a new bride. The paymaster put the full amount of six rupees in her hand.

She was stupefied. Surely the paymaster was mistaken! In these three years she had never once got her full pay. And now to get even half would have been a windfall. She stood there for a second in case the paymaster should ask for the money back. When he asked her, 'Why are you standing here now, why don't you move along?' she said softly, 'But it's the full amount.'

Puzzled the paymaster looked at her and said, 'What else do you want—do you want to get less?'

'There's no penalty deducted?'

'No, today there aren't any deductions.'

She came away but in her heart she was not content. She was full of remorse for having abused the Inspector.

A Lesson in the Holy Life*

DOMESTIC SQUABBLES AND A DEARTH OF INVITATIONS led Pandit Chintamani to consider renouncing the world and when he vowed to become a wandering ascetic his best friend, Pandit Moteram Shastri, gave him this advice.

'Friend, I've been intimately acquainted with a good many first-class mahatmas. Now, when they arrive at some well-to-do citizen's door they don't fall in a heap and hold out their hands and call down hypocritical blessings such as "God keep you in body and soul, may you always be happy." Such is the way of beggars. As soon as a holy man reaches the door he lets out his war-cry in a regular yell so that everybody inside the house is astonished and comes running to see what's happened. I know two or three of these slogans—you can use any you like. Gudri *Baba* used to say, "If anybody dies five will die!" When they heard this battle-cry people would fall right at his feet. Siddh Bhagat had a fine slogan: "Eat, drink and be merry but watch out for the holy man's stick." Nanga Baba would say, "Give to me, feed me, let me drink, let me sleep." Just remember, your prestige depends a good deal on your slogan. What else can I tell you? Don't forget, you and I have been friends for a long time, we've enjoyed the same free dinners hundreds of times. Whenever we were at the

---

*Guru-Mantra

same banquet we used to compete to eat up one dish more than the other. I'm going to miss you! May God give you a happy life.'

Chintamani wasn't pleased with any of the slogans. He said, 'Think up some special cry for me.'

'All right—how's this one: "If you don't give to me I'll run you into the ground."'

'Yes, I like that one, but if you'll allow me, I'll shorten it.'

'Go right ahead.'

'Then how about this: "Give or I'll run you into the ground."'

Moteram leaped up. 'By the Lord above, that's absolutely unique! Devotion has illuminated you. Splendid! Now try it out just once and we'll see how you do it.'

Chintamani stuck his fingers in his ears and yelled with all his might. 'Give or I'll run you into the ground!' The noise was so thunderous that even Moteram was startled. The bats flew out of the trees in dismay and dogs began to bark.

Moteram said, 'Friend, your cry was like the roar of a lion. Now your slogan has been decided, I have a few other things to tell you, so pay attention. The language of holy men is quite different from our ordinary way of speaking. We say "Sir," for example, to some people, and just "you" to others. But the holy man says "thou" to everybody, important or insignificant, rich or poor, old or young; however, go on treating old people with respect. Also remember never to talk plain Hindi. Otherwise the secret will be out that you're an ordinary Brahman and not a real holy man. Make your language fancy. To say, for example, "My good woman, give me something to eat" is not the style of the holy man. A genuine mahatma will say it like this: "Woman, spread a feast before me, and you will be walking in the paths of righteousness."'

'Friend,' Chintamani said, 'how can I praise you enough? You've helped me beyond measure.'

Having given this advice, Moteram took his leave. Chintamani set out and what should he see right away but a crowd of holy men sitting in front of a *bhang* and hashish shop smoking hashish. When they saw Chintamani one of the holy men pronounced his slogan:

'Move along, move along,
Otherwise, I'll prove you wrong.'

Another holy man proclaimed:

'Fee fi fo fum
We holy men have finally come,
From now on only fun.'

While these syllables were still echoing in the skies a third mahatma
roared out:

'Here and there
down and up
Hurry up and fill my cup.'

Chintamani could not restrain himself. He burst out with 'Give or
I'll run you into the ground!'

As soon as they heard this the holy men greeted him. The bowl of the hookah was refilled at once and the task of lighting it was assigned to Pandit Chintamani. He thought, if I don't accept the pipe my secret will be out. Nervously he took it. Now anyone who has never smoked hashish can try and try without being able to make the pipe draw. Closing his eyes Chintamani inhaled with all his might. The pipe fell from his hands, his eyes popped, he foamed at the mouth but not the least bit of smoke came from his lips nor was there any sign that the pipe was kindled. This lack of know-how was quite enough to ruin his standing in the society of holy men. A couple of them advanced angrily and roughly catching him by the hands, pulled him up.

'A curse on you,' one said, and another, 'Aren't you ashamed of pretending to be a mahatma?'

Humiliated, Panditji went and sat down near a sweets shop and the holy men, striking tambourines, began to sing this hymn:

> 'Illusion is the world, beloved, the world is an illusion.
> Both sin and holiness are lies—there's the philosophical solution.
> The world is all illusion.
> A curse on those who forbid us bhang and hashish,
> Krishna, lover, all the world's illusion.'

Festival of Eid*

A FULL THIRTY DAYS AFTER RAMADAN COMES EID. HOW wonderful and beautiful is the morning of Eid! The trees look greener, the field more festive, the sky has a lovely pink glow. Look at the sun! It comes up brighter and more dazzling than before to wish the world a very happy Eid. The village is agog with excitement. Everyone is up early to go to the Eidgah mosque. One finds a button missing from his shirt and is hurrying to his neighbour's house for thread and needle. Another finds that the leather of his shoes has become hard and is running to the oil-press for oil to grease it. They are dumping fodder before their oxen because by the time they get back from the Eidgah it may be late afternoon. It is a good three miles from the village. There will also be hundreds of people to greet and chat with; they would certainly not be finished before midday.

The boys are more excited than the others. Some of them kept only one fast—and that only till noon. Some didn't even do that. But no one can stop them from going to the Eidgah. Fasting is for the grown-ups and the aged. For the boys it is only the day of Eid. They have been talking about it all the time. And now they are impatient with people for not hurrying up. They have no concern with things that have to be done. They are not bothered whether

*Idgah

or not there is enough milk and sugar for the vermicelli pudding. All they want is to eat the pudding. Their pockets bulge with coins. They are forever taking the treasure out of their pockets, counting and recounting it before putting it back. Mahmood counts 'One, two, ten, twelve'—he has twelve pice. Mohsin has 'One, two, three, eight, nine, fifteen' pice. Out of this countless hoard they will buy countless things: toys, sweets, paper-pipes, rubber balls—and much else.

The happiest of the boys is Hamid. He is only four; poorly dressed, thin and famished-looking. His father died last year of cholera. Then his mother wasted away and, without anyone finding out what had ailed her, she also died. Now Hamid sleeps in Granny Ameena's lap and is as happy as a lark. She tells him that his father has gone to earn money and will return with sack-loads of silver. And that his mother has gone to Allah to get lovely gifts for him. This makes Hamid very happy. Hamid has no shoes on his feet; the cap on his head is soiled and tattered; its gold thread has turned black. Nevertheless, Hamid is happy. He knows that when his father comes back with sacks full of silver and his mother with gifts from Allah he will be able to fulfil all his heart's desires. Then he will have more than Mahmood, Mohsin, Noorey, and Sammi.

In her hovel the unfortunate Ameena sheds bitter tears. It is Eid and she does not have even a handful of grain. Hamid goes to his grandmother and says, 'Granny, don't you fret over me! I will be the first to get back. Don't worry!'

Ameena is sad. Other boys are going out with their fathers. She is the only 'father' Hamid has. How can she let him go to the fair all by himself? What if he gets lost in the crowd? How can he walk three miles? He doesn't even have a pair of shoes. He will get blisters on his feet. If she went along with him she could pick him up now and then. But then who would be there to cook the vermicelli?

The villagers leave in one party. With the boys is Hamid. They run on ahead of the elders and wait for them under a tree. Why do the oldies drag their feet? And Hamid is like one with wings on his feet. How could anyone think he would get tired?

They reach the suburbs of the town. On both sides of the road are mansions of the rich enclosed all around by thick, high walls. In the gardens, mango and *leechee* trees are laden with fruit. A boy hurls a stone at a mango tree. The gardener rushes out screaming abuse at them. By then the boys are furlongs out of his reach and roaring with laughter. What a silly ass they make of the gardener!

Soon the boys proceed to the stores of the sweetmeat vendors. All so gaily decorated! Who can eat all these delicacies? Just look! Every store has them piled up in mountain heaps.

They say that after nightfall, Jinns come and buy up everything. 'My Abba says that at midnight there is a Jinn at every stall. He has all that remains weighed and pays in real rupees, just the sort of rupees we have,' says Mohsin.

Hamid is not convinced. 'Where would the Jinns find rupees?'

'Jinns are never short of money,' replies Mohsin. 'They can get into any treasury they want. Mister, don't you know no iron bars can stop them? They have all the diamonds and rubies they want. If they are pleased with anyone they will give him baskets full of diamonds. They are here one moment and five minutes later they can be in Calcutta.'

Hamid asks again, 'Are these Jinns very big?'

'Each one is as big as the sky,' asserts Mohsin. 'He has his feet on the ground, his head touches the sky. But if he so wanted, he could get into a tiny brass pot.'

'How do people make Jinns happy?' asks Hamid. 'If anyone taught me the secret, I would make at least one Jinn happy with me.'

'I do not know,' replies Mohsin, 'but the Chaudhri Sahib has a lot of Jinns under his control. If anything is stolen, he can trace it and even tell you the name of the thief. Jinns tell him everything that is going on in the world.'

Hamid understands how Chaudhri Sahib has become so rich and why people hold him in so much respect.

At long last the Eidgah comes in view. Above it are massive tamarind
trees casting their shade on the cemented floor on which carpets have
been spread. And there are row-upon-row of worshippers as far as the
eye can see, spilling well beyond the mosque courtyard.
Newcomers line themselves behind the others. Here
neither wealth nor status matters because in the eyes
of Islam all men are equal. Our villagers wash their
hands and feet and make their own line behind
the others. What a beautiful, heart-moving sight
it is! What perfect coordination of movements!
A hundred thousand heads bow together in prayer! And
then all together they stand erect; bow down
and sit on their knees! Many times they
repeat these movements—exactly as if
a hundred thousand electric bulbs
were switched on and off at the same
time again and again. What a wonderful spectacle it is!

The prayer is over. Men embrace each other. They descend on the
sweet and toy-vendors' stores like an army moving to an assault. In
this matter the grown-up rustic is no less eager than the boys.
Look, here is a swing! Pay a pice and enjoy riding up to the
heavens and then plummeting down to the earth. And here is
the roundabout strung with wooden elephants, horses, and
camels! Pay one pice and have twenty-five rounds of fun.
Mahmood and Mohsin and Noorey and other boys mount the
horses and camels.

Hamid watches them from a distance. All he has are three pice. He
couldn't afford to part with a third of his treasure for a few
miserable rounds.

They've finished with the roundabouts; now it is time for the toys.
There is a row of stalls on one side with all kinds of toys: soldiers
and milkmaids, kings and ministers, water-carriers and
washerwomen and holy men. Splendid display! How lifelike!
Mahmood buys a policeman in khaki with a red turban on his
head and a gun on his shoulder. Looks as if he is marching in a
parade. Mohsin likes the water-carrier with his back bent under

the weight of the water-bag. He holds the handle of the bag in one hand and looks pleased with himself. It seems as if the water is about to pour out of the bag. Noorey has fallen for the lawyer. What an expression of learning he has on his face! A black gown over a long, white coat with a gold watch chain going into a pocket, a fat volume of some law book in his hand. Appears as if he has just finished arguing a case in a court of law.

These toys cost two pice each. All Hamid has are three pice; how can he afford to buy such expensive toys? If they dropped out of his hand, they would be smashed to bits. If a drop of water fell on them, the paint would run. What would he do with toys like these? They'd be of no use to him.

Mohsin says, 'My water-carrier will sprinkle water every day, morning and evening.'

Mahmood says, 'My policeman will guard my house. If a thief comes near, he will shoot him with his gun.'

Noorey says, 'My lawyer will fight my cases.'

Sammi says, 'My washer-woman will wash my clothes every day.'

Hamid pooh-poohs their toys. They're made of clay—one fall and they'll break in pieces. But his eyes look at them hungrily and he wishes he could hold them in his hands for just a moment or two. But young boys are not givers, particularly when it is something new. Poor Hamid doesn't get to touch the toys.

After the toys it is sweets. Someone buys sesame seed candy, others *gulab-jamuns* or *halva*. They smack their lips with relish. Only Hamid is left out. The luckless boy has at least three pice; why doesn't he also buy something to eat? He looks with hungry eyes at the others.

After the sweet-vendors, there are a few hardware stores and shops of real and artificial jewellery. There is nothing there to attract the boys' attention. So they go ahead—all of them except Hamid who stops to see a pile of tongs. It occurs to him that his granny does not have a pair of tongs. Each time she bakes *chapattis*, the iron plate burns her hands. If he were to buy her a pair of tongs she would be

very pleased. She would never burn her fingers; it would be a useful thing to have in the house. What use are toys? They are a waste of money. You can have some fun with them but only for a very short time. Then you forget all about them.

Hamid's friends have gone ahead. They are at a stall drinking sherbet. How selfish they are! They bought so many sweets but did not give him one. And then they want him to play with them; they want him to do odd jobs for them. Now if any of them asked him to do something, he would tell them, 'Go suck your lollipop, it will burn your mouth; it will give you a rash of pimples and boils; your tongue will always crave for sweets; you will have to steal money to buy them and get a thrashing in the bargain. It's all written in books. Nothing will happen to my tongs. No sooner my granny sees my pair of tongs she will run up to take it from me and say, "My child has brought me a pair of tongs," and shower me with a thousand blessings. She will show it off to the neighbours' womenfolk. Soon the whole village will be saying, "Hamid has brought his granny a pair of tongs, how nice he is!" No one will bless the other boys for the toys they have got for themselves. Blessings of elders are heard in the court of Allah and are immediately acted on. One day my father will return. And also my mother. Then I will ask these chaps, "Do you want any toys? How many?" I will give each one a basket full of toys and teach them how to treat friends. I am not the sort who buys a pica worth of lollipops to tease others by sucking them myself. I know they will laugh and say Hamid has brought a pair of tongs. They can go to the Devil!'

Hamid asks the shopkeeper, 'How much for this pair of tongs?'

The shopkeeper looks at him and seeing no older person with him replies, 'It's not for you.'

'Is it for sale or not?'

'Why should it not be for sale? Why else should I have bothered to bring it here?'

'Why don't you then tell me how much it is!'

'It will cost you six pice.'

Hamid's heart sinks. 'Let me have the correct price.'

'All right, it will be five pice, bottom price. Take it or leave it.' Hamid steels his heart and says, 'Will you give it to me for three?' And proceeds to walk away lest the shopkeeper screams at him. But the shopkeeper does not scream. He calls Hamid back and gives him the pair of tongs. Hamid carries it on his shoulder as if it were a gun and struts up proudly to show it to his friends. Let us hear what they have to say.

Mohsin laughs and says, 'Are you crazy? What will you do with the tongs?' Hamid flings the tongs on the ground and replies, 'Try and throw your water-carrier on the ground. Every bone in his body will break.'

Mahmood says, 'Are these tongs some kind of toy?'

'Why not?' retorts Hamid. 'Place them across your shoulders and it is a gun; wield them in your hands and it is like the tongs carried by singing mendicants—they can make the same clanging as a pair of cymbals. One smack and they will reduce all your toys to dust. And much as your toys may try they could not bend a hair on the head of my tongs. My tongs are like a brave tiger.'

Sammi who had bought a small tambourine asks, 'Will you exchange them for my tambourine? It is worth eight pice.'

Hamid pretends not to look at the tambourine. 'My tongs if they wanted to could tear out the bowels of your tambourine. All it has is a leather skin and all it can say is dhub, dhub. A drop of water could silence it forever. My brave pair of tongs can weather water and storms, without budging an inch.'

The pair of tongs wins over everyone to its side. But now no one has any money left and the fairground has been left far behind. It is well past nine and the sun is getting hotter every minute. Everyone is in a hurry to get home. Even if they talked their fathers into it, they could not get the tongs. This Hamid is a bit of a rascal. He saved up his money for the tongs.

Mohsin puts all he has in his plea, 'But your tongs cannot go and fetch water, can they?'

Hamid raises the tongs and replies, 'One angry word of command from my tongs and your water-carrier will hasten to fetch the water and sprinkle it at any doorstep he is ordered to.'

Mohsin has no answer. Mahmood comes to his rescue. 'If we are caught, we are caught. We will have to do the rounds of the law courts in chains. Then we will be at the lawyer's feet asking for help.'

Hamid has no answer to this powerful argument. He asks, 'Who will come to arrest us?'

Noorey puffs out his chest and replies, 'This policeman with the gun.'

Hamid makes a face and says with scorn, 'This wretch come to arrest the Champion of India! Okay, let's have it out over a bout of wrestling. Far from catching them, he will be scared to look at my tongs in the face.'

Mohsin thinks of another ploy. 'Your tongs' face will burn in the fire every day.' He is sure that this will leave Hamid speechless. That is not so. Pat comes Hamid with the retort, 'Mister, it is only the brave who can jump into a fire. Your miserable lawyers, policemen, and water-carriers will run into their homes. Only this Champion of India can leap into the fire.'

Mahmood has one more try, 'The lawyer will have chairs to sit and tables for his things. Your tongs will only have the kitchen floor to lie on.'

Hamid cannot think of an appropriate retort so he says whatever comes into his mind, 'The tongs won't stay in the kitchen. When your lawyer sits on his chair my tongs will knock him down on the ground.'

It does not make sense but our three heroes are utterly squashed—almost as if a champion kite had been brought down from the heavens to the earth by a cheap, miserable paper imitation. Thus Hamid wins the field. His tongs are the Champion of India. Neither Mohsin nor Mahmood, neither Noorey nor Sammi—nor anyone else can dispute the fact.

No one can deny that toys are unreliable things: they break, while Hamid's tongs will remain as they are for years.

The boys begin to make terms of peace. Mohsin says, 'Give me your tongs for a while, you can have my water-carrier for the same time.'

Both Mahmood and Noorey similarly offer their toys. Hamid has no hesitation in agreeing to these terms. The tongs pass from one hand to another; and the toys are in turn handed to Hamid. How lovely they are!

Hamid tries to wipe the tears of his defeated adversaries. 'I was simply pulling your leg, honestly I was. How can these tongs made of iron compare with your toys?' But Mohsin's party are not solaced. The tongs have won the day and no amount of water can wash away their stamp of authority. Mohsin says, 'No one will bless us for these toys.'

Mahmood adds, 'You talk of blessings! We may get a thrashing instead. My Amma is bound to say, "Are these clay toys all that you could find at the fair?"'

Hamid has to concede that no mother will be as pleased with the toys as his granny will be when she sees the tongs. All he had was three pice and he has no reason to regret the way he has spent them. And now his tongs are the Champion of India and king of toys.

By eleven the village was again agog with excitement. All those who had gone to the fair were back at home. Mohsin's little sister ran up, wrenched the water-carrier out of his hands, and began to dance with joy. Mister Water-carrier slipped out of her hand, fell on the ground and went to paradise. The brother and sister began to fight; and both had lots to cry about. Their mother lost her temper because of the racket they were making and gave each two resounding slaps.

Noorey's lawyer met an end befitting his grand status. A lawyer could not sit on the ground. He had to keep his dignity in mind. Two nails were driven into the wall, a plank put on them and a carpet of paper spread on the plank. The honourable counsel was seated like a king on his throne. Noorey began to wave a fan over him. He knew that in the law courts there were *khus* curtains and electric fans. So the least he could do was to provide a hand fan, otherwise the hot legal arguments might affect his lawyer's brains. Noorey was waving his fan made of bamboo leaf, when the poor lawyer got knocked off his throne, fell on the ground and mingled with the dust.

Mahmood's policeman remained. He was immediately put on duty to guard the village. But this police constable was no ordinary mortal who could walk on his own two feet. He had to be provided a palanquin. This was a basket lined with tatters of discarded clothes of red colour for the policeman to recline in comfort. Mahmood picked up the basket and started on his rounds. His two younger brothers followed him lisping, 'Shopkeepers, keep awake!' But night has to be dark; Mahmood stumbled, the basket slipped out of his hand. Mr Constable with his gun crashed on the ground. He was short of one leg.

Now let's hear what happened to our friend Hamid. As soon as she heard his voice, Granny Ameena ran out of the house, picked him up and kissed him. Suddenly she noticed the tongs in his hand. 'Where did you find these tongs?'

'I bought them.'

'How much did you pay for them?'

'Three pice.'

Granny Ameena beat her breast. 'You are a stupid child! It is almost noon and you haven't had anything to eat or drink. And what do you buy—tongs! Couldn't you find anything better in the fair than this pair of iron tongs?'

Hamid replied in injured tones, 'You burn your fingers on the iron plate. That is why I bought them.'

The old woman's temper suddenly changed to love. What a selfless child! What concern for others! What a big heart! How he must have suffered seeing other boys buying toys and gobbling sweets! Even at the fair he thought of his old grandmother. Granny Ameena's heart was too full for words.

She spread her apron and beseeched Allah's blessings for her grandchild. Big tears fell from her eyes. How was Hamid to understand what was going on inside her!

A Car-Splashing*

WELL, IT'S LIKE THIS: EARLY IN THE MORNING I FINISH OFF MY bath and my prayers, paint a vermillion circle on my forehead, get into my yellow robe and wooden sandals, tuck my astrological charts under my arm, grab hold of my stick—a regular skull-cracker—and start out for a client's house. I was supposed to settle the right day for a wedding; it was going to earn me at least a rupee. Over and above the breakfast. And my breakfast is no ordinary breakfast. Common clerks don't have the courage to invite me to a meal. A whole month of breakfasts for them is just one day's meal for me. In this connection I fully appreciate rich gentlemen and bankers—how they feed you, how they feed you! So generously that you feel happy all over! After I get an idea of the generosity of the client I accept his invitation. If somebody puts on a long face when it's time to feed me I lose my appetite. How can anybody feed you if he's weeping? I can't digest a meal like that at all. I like a client who hails me with, 'Hey Shastriji, have some sweets!' whom I can answer, 'No, friend—not yet.'

It had rained a lot during the night. There were puddles everywhere on the road. I was walking along all wrapped up in my thoughts when a car came along splashing through the puddles. My face got spattered. And then what do I see but my *dhoti* looking as

*Motor Ke Chinte

though somebody mixed up a mess of mud and flung it all over it. My clothes were ruined; apart from that, I was filthy, to say nothing of the money lost. If I'd caught those people in the car I'd have done a job on them they wouldn't forget. I stood there, helpless. I couldn't go to a client's house in this state and my own house was at least a full mile away. The people in the street were all clapping to ridicule me. I never was in such a mess. Well, old heart, what are you going to do now? If you go home what will the wife say?

I decided in a trice what my duty was. I got together about a dozen stones from all around and waited for the next car. I'd show them a Brahman's power.

It wasn't even ten minutes before a car came into sight. Oh no! It was the same car. He'd probably gone to get the master from the station and was returning home. As soon as it got close I let fly a rock. I shot it out with all my strength. The gentleman's cap went flying and landed on the side of the road. The car slowed down. I fired again. The window-pane smashed to pieces and one piece even landed on the fine gentleman's cheek drawing blood. The car stopped and the gentleman got out and came toward me, gave me a punch and said, 'You swine, I'll take you to the police!' I'd scarcely heard him when, throwing my books down on the ground, I grabbed him by the waist, tripped him and he fell with a smack in the mud. I jumped on top of him at once and gave him a good twenty punches one after the other until he got dizzy. In the mean-time his wife got out. High-heeled shoes, silk sari, powdered cheeks, lipstick, mascara. She began to poke at me with her umbrella. I left the husband and wielding my stick said, 'Lady, don't meddle in men's business or you may get a whack and a bruise and I'd be very sorry about that.'

The gentleman found the occasion to pick himself up and give me a kick with his booted feet. I got a real knock in the knee. Losing patience, I struck out with my stick, getting him in the legs. He fell like a tree when you chop it down. Memsahib came running brandishing her umbrella. I took it away from her without any trouble and threw it away. The driver had been sitting in the car all this time. Now he got out too and came rushing at me with a cane. I brought my stick down on him too and he fell flat. A whole mob had gathered to see the fun. Still lying on the ground the sahib said, 'You rogue, we'll hand you over to the police!'

I wielded my stick again and wanted to thump him on the skull but he folded his hands and said, 'No, no, *baba*, we won't go to the police. Forgive me.'

I said, 'All right, leave the police out of it or I'll crack you over the skull. I'd get six months at the most for it but I'd break you of the habit. You drive along and splash up mud and you're blind with conceit. You don't give a damn who's in front of you or alongside of you.'

One of the onlookers said, '*Arrey*, Maharaj! These drivers know perfectly well they're splashing and when some man gets drenched they think it's great fun and laugh at him. You did well to give one of them a lesson.'

'You hear what the people are saying?' I shouted at the sahib. He gave a dirty look toward the man who'd spoken and said to him, 'You're lying, it's a complete lie.'

'You're still just as rude, are you! Shall I have another go at you with the stick?'

'No, baba,' he said humbly. 'It's true, it's true. Now are you satisfied?'

Another bystander said, 'He'll tell you what you want to hear now but as soon as he's back in his automobile he'll start the same old business all over again. Just put 'em in their cars and they all think they're related to the maharaja.'

'Tell him to admit he's wrong,' said another.

'No, no, make him hold on to his ears and do knee-bends.'

'And what about the driver? They're all rogues. If a rich man's puffed up, that's one thing, but what are you drivers so conceited about? They take hold of the wheel and they can't see straight any more.'

I accepted the suggestion that master and driver hold on to their ears and do knee-bends, the way you punish little children, while Memsahib counted. 'Listen, memsahib,' I said, 'you've got to count a whole hundred bends, not one less but as many over as you like.'

Two men drew the master up by his hands, two others that gentleman-driver. The poor driver's leg was bruised but he began to do the knee-bends. The master was still pretty cocky; he lay down and began to spew out gibberish. I was furious and swore in my heart that I wouldn't let him go without doing a hundred knee-bends. I ordered four men to shove the car off the edge of the road.

They set to work at once. Instead of four, fifty men crowded around and began to shove the car. The road was built up very high with the land below it on either side. If the car had slid down it would have smashed to pieces. The car had already reached the edge of the road when the sahib let out a groan and stood up and said, 'Baba, don't wreck my car, we'll do the knee-bends.'

I ordered the men to stand off. But they were all enjoying themselves and nobody paid any attention to me. But when I lifted up the stick and ran for them they all abandoned the car and the sahib, shutting his eyes, began to do the knee-bends.

After ten of them I said to the Memsahib, 'How many has he done?'

Very snooty, she said, 'I wasn't counting.'

'Then sahib's going to be groaning and moaning all day long, I won't let him go. If you want to take him home in good health count the knee-bends, then I'll let him go.'

The sahib saw that without his punishment he wouldn't get away with his life, so he began the knee-bends again. One, two, three, four, five...

Suddenly another car came into view. Sahib saw it and said very humbly, 'Panditji, take pity on me, you are my father. Take pity on me and I won't sit in a car again.'

I felt merciful and said, 'No, I don't forbid you to sit in your car, I just want you to treat men like men when you're in it.'

The second car was speeding along. I gave a signal. All the men picked up rocks. The owner of this car was doing the driving

himself. Slowing down he tried to creep through us gradually when I advanced and caught him by the ears, shook him violently and after giving him a slap on both cheeks, said, 'Don't splash with the car, understand? Move along politely.' But he began to gabble until he saw a hundred men carrying rocks, then without any more fuss he went on his way.

A minute after he left another car came along. I ordered fifty men to bar the road; the car stopped. I gave him a few slaps too but the poor fellow was a gentleman. He took them as though he enjoyed them and continued his journey.

Suddenly a man said, 'The police are coming.'

And everybody took to his heels. I too came down off the road and sidling into a little lane I disappeared.

The Story of Two Bullocks*

JHURI THE VEGETABLE FARMER HAD TWO BULLOCKS NAMED Hira and Moti. Both were of fine Pachai stock, of great stature, beautiful to behold, and diligent at their labours.

The two had lived together for a very long time and become sworn brothers. Face to face or side by side they would hold discussions in their silent language. How each understood the other's thoughts we cannot say, but they certainly possessed some mysterious power. They would express their love by licking and sniffing one another, and sometimes they would even lock horns— not from hostility but rather out of friendship and a sense of fun, the way friends as soon as they become intimate slap and pummel one another; any friendship lacking such displays seems rather superficial and insipid and not to be trusted. When they were released from the yoke after their day's work at noon or in the evening they would lick and nuzzle one another to ease their fatigue. When the oilseed cake and straw was tossed into the manger they would stand up together, thrust their muzzles into the trough together, and sit down side by side. When one withdrew his mouth the other would do so too.

On one occasion Jhuri sent the pair to his father-in-law's. How could the bullocks know why they were being sent away? They assumed that the master had sold them. If God had given them

Do Bailon Ki Katha

speech, they would have asked Jhuri, 'Why are you throwing us poor wretches out? We've done everything possible to serve you well. If working as hard as we did couldn't get the job done, you could have made us work still harder. We were willing to die labouring for you. We never complained about the food, whatever you gave us to eat we bowed our heads and ate it, so why did you sell us into the hands of this tyrant?'

At evening the two bullocks reached their new place, hungry after a whole day without food, but when they were brought to the manger, neither so much as stuck his mouth in. Their hearts were heavy; they were separated from the home they had thought was their own. New house, new village, new people, all seemed alien to them.

They consulted in their mute language, glancing at one another out of the corners of their eyes, and lay down. When the village was deep in sleep the two of them pulled hard, broke their tether and set out for home. That tether was very tough, no one could have guessed that any bullock could break it; but a redoubled power had entered into them and the ropes snapped with one violent jerk.

When he got up early in the morning Jhuri saw that his two bullocks were standing at the trough, half a tether dangling from each of their necks. Their legs were muddied up to the knees and resentful love gleamed in their eyes.

When Jhuri saw the bullocks he was overwhelmed with affection for them. He ran and threw his arms around their necks, and very pleasant was the spectacle of that loving embrace and kissing.

The children of the household and the village boys gathered, clapping their hands in welcome.

One boy said, 'Nobody has bullocks like these,' and another agreed, 'They came back from so far all by themselves,' while a third said, 'They're not bullocks, in an earlier life they were men.' And nobody dared disagree with this.

But when Jhuri's wife saw the bullocks at the gate she got angry and said, 'What loafers these oxen are, they didn't work at my father's place for one day before they ran away!'

Jhuri could not listen to his bullocks being slandered like this. 'Loafers, are they? At your father's they must not have fed them so what were they to do?'

In her overbearing way his wife said, 'Oh sure, you're the only one who knows how to feed bullocks while everybody else gives them nothing but water.'

Jhuri railed at her, 'If they'd been fed why would they run off?'

Aggravated, she said, 'They ran away just because those people don't make fools of themselves spoiling them like you. They feed them but they also make them work hard. These two are real lazy-bones and they ran away. Let's see them get oilseed and bran now! I'll give them nothing but dry straw, they can eat it or drop dead.'

So it came about. The hired hand was given strict orders to feed them nothing but dry straw.

When the bullocks put their faces in the trough they found it insipid. No savour, no juice—how could they eat it? With eyes full of hope they began to stare toward the door.

Jhuri said to the hired hand, 'Why the devil don't you throw in a little oilseed?'

'The mistress would surely kill me.'

'Then do it on the sly.'

'Oh no, boss, afterwards you'll side with her.'

The next day Jhuri's brother-in-law came again and took the bullocks away. This time he yoked them to the wagon.

A couple of times Moti wanted to knock the wagon into the ditch, but Hira, who was more tolerant, held him back.

When they reached the house, Gaya tied them with thick ropes and paid them back for yesterday's mischief. Again he threw down the same dry straw. To his own bullocks he gave oilseed cake, ground lentils, everything.

The two bullocks had never suffered such an insult. Jhuri wouldn't strike them even with a flower stem. The two of them would rise up at a click of his tongue, while here they were beaten. Along with the pain of injured pride they had to put up with dry straw. They didn't even bother to look in the trough.

The next day Gaya yoked them to the plow, but it was as though the two of them had sworn an oath not to lift a foot—he grew tired beating them but not one foot would they lift. One time when the cruel fellow delivered a sharp blow on Hira's nostrils Moti's anger went out of control and he took to his heels with the plow. Plough-share, rope, yoke, harness, all were smashed to pieces. Had there not been strong ropes around their necks it would have been impossible to catch the two of them.

Hira said in his silent language, 'It's useless to run away.'

Moti answered, 'But he was going to kill you.'

'We'll really get beaten now.'

'So what? We were born bullocks, how can we escape beating?'

'Gaya's coming on the run with a couple of men and they're both carrying sticks.'

Moti said. 'Just say the word and I'll show them a little fun. Here he comes with his stick!'

'No, brother!' Hira cautioned. 'Just stand still.'

'If he beats me I'll knock one or two of them down.'

'No, that's not the *dharma* of our community.'

Moti could only stand, protesting violently in his heart. Gaya arrived, caught them and took them away. Fortunately he didn't beat them this time, for if he had Moti would have struck back. When they saw his fierce look Gaya and his helpers concluded that this time it would be best to put it off.

This day again the same dry straw was brought to them. They stood in silence. In the house the people were eating dinner. Just then a quite young girl came out carrying a couple of pieces of bread. She fed the two of them and went away. How could a piece of bread still their hunger? But in their hearts they felt as though they had been fed a full meal. Here too was the dwelling of some gentle folk. The girl was Bharo's daughter; her mother was dead and her stepmother beat her often, so that she felt a kind of sympathy for the bullocks.

The two were yoked all day, took a lot of beatings, got stubborn. In the evening they were tied up in their stall, and at night the same little girl would come out and feed some bread to each of them. The happy result of this communion of love was that even though they ate only a few mouthfuls of the dry straw they did not grow weak; still their eyes and every cell of their bodies filled with rebelliousness.

One day Moti said in his silent language, 'I can't stand it any longer, Hira. So what do you say, tonight we'll break the ropes and run away?'

'Yes, I'll agree to that, but how can we break such a thick rope?'

'There *is* a way. First gnaw the rope a bit, then it will snap with one jerk.'

At night when the girl had fed them and gone off the two began to gnaw their ropes, but the thick cord wouldn't fit in their mouths. The poor fellows tried hard over and over again without any luck.

Suddenly the door of the house opened and the same girl came out; the bullocks lowered their heads and began to lick her hand. Their tails stood up while she stroked their foreheads, and then she said, 'I'm going to let you go. Be very quiet and run away or these people will kill you. In the house today they were talking about putting rings in your noses.'

She untied the rope, but the two stood silent.

'Well, let's go,' said Hira, 'only tomorrow this orphan's going to be in a lot of trouble. Everybody in the house will suspect her.'

Suddenly the girl yelled, 'Uncle's bullocks are running away! Daddy, daddy, come quick, they're running away!'

Gaya came rushing out of the house to catch the bullocks. They were running now, with Gaya fast behind them. They ran even faster and Gaya set up a shout. Then he turned back to fetch some men of the village. This was the chance for the two friends to make good their escape, and they ran straight ahead, no longer aware by now just where they were. There was no trace of the familiar road they'd come by. They were coming to villages they'd never seen. Then the two of them halted at the edge of a field and began to think about what they ought to do now.

Hira said, 'It appears we've lost our way.'

'You took to your heels without thinking. We should have knocked him down dead right on the spot.'

'If we'd killed him what would the world say? He abandoned his dharma, but we stuck to ours.'

They were dizzy with hunger. Peas were growing in the field and they began to browse, stopping occasionally to listen for anyone coming.

They had scarcely eaten a couple of mouthfuls when two men with sticks came running and surrounded the two friends. Hira was on the embankment and slipped away, but Moti was down in the soggy field. His hooves were so deep in mud that he couldn't run, and he was caught. When Hira saw his comrade in trouble he dashed back. If they were going to be trapped, then they'd be trapped together. So the watchmen caught him too.

Early in the morning the two friends were shut up in a village pound.

The two friends stayed tied up there for a week. No one gave them so much as a bit of hay. True, water *was* given to them once. This was all their nourishment. They got so weak that they could not even stand up, and their ribs were sticking out.

One day someone beat a drum outside the enclosure and towards noon about fifty or sixty people gathered there. Then the two friends were brought out and the inspection began. People came and studied their appearance and went away disappointed. Who would buy bullocks that looked like corpses?

Suddenly there came a bearded man with red eyes and a cruel face; he dug his fingers into the haunches of the bullocks and began to talk with the clerk. When they saw his expression the hearts of the two friends grew weak from what their intuition told them. They had no doubt at all as to who he was and why he felt them with his hands. They looked at one another with frightened eyes and lowered their heads.

Hira said, 'We ran away from Gaya's house in vain. We won't survive this.'

Without much faith Moti answered, 'They say God has mercy on everybody. Why isn't He being merciful to us?'

'To God it's all the same whether we live or die. Don't worry, it's not so bad, for a little while we'll be with Him. Once He saved us in the shape of that little girl, so won't He save us now?'

'This man is going to cut our throats. Just watch.'

'So why worry? Every bit of us, flesh, hide, horns and bones, will be used for something or the other.'

When the auction was over the friends went off with that bearded man. Every bit of their bodies was trembling. They could scarcely lift their feet, but they were so frightened they managed to keep stumbling along—for if they slowed down the least bit they'd get a good whack from the stick.

Along the way they saw a herd of cows and bullocks grazing in a verdant meadow. All the animals were happy, sleek and supple. Some were leaping about, others lying down contentedly chewing their cud. What a happy life was theirs! Yet how selfish they all were. Not one of them cared about how their two brothers must be suffering after falling into the hands of the butcher.

Suddenly it seemed to them that the road was familiar. Yes, this was the road by which Gaya had taken them away. They were coming to the same fields and orchards, the same villages. At every instant their pace quickened. All their fatigue and weakness disappeared. Oh, just look, here was their own meadow, here was the same well where they had worked the winch to pull up the bucket, yes, it was the same well.

Moti said, 'Our house is close by!'

'It's God's mercy!' said Hira.

'As for me, I'm making a run for home!'

'Will he let us go?'

'I'll knock him down and kill him.'

'No, no, run and make it to our stalls, and we won't budge from there.'

As though they'd gone crazy, joyfully kicking up their heels like calves, they made off for the house. There was their stall! They ran and stood by it while the bearded man came dashing after them.

Jhuri was sitting in his doorway sunning himself. As soon as he saw the bullocks he ran and embraced them over and over again. Tears of joy flowed from the two friends' eyes, and one of them licked Jhuri's hand.

The bearded man came up and grabbed their tethers.

'These are my bullocks,' said Jhuri.

'How can they be? I just bought them at auction at the cattle pound.'

'I'll bet you stole them,' said Jhuri. 'Just shut up and leave. They're *my* bullocks. They'll be sold only when *I* sell them. Who has the right to auction off my bullocks?'

Said the bearded man, 'I'll go to the police station and make a complaint.'

'They're my bullocks, the proof is they came and stood at my door.'

In a rage the bearded man stepped forward to drag the bullocks away. This is when Moti lowered his horns. The bearded man stepped back. Moti charged and the man took to his heels, with Moti after him, and stopped only at the outskirts of the village where he took his stand guarding the road. The butcher stopped at some distance, yelled back threats and insults and threw stones. And Moti stood blocking his path like a victorious hero. The villagers came out to watch the entertainment and had a good laugh.

When the bearded man acknowledged defeat and went away Moti came back strutting.

Hira said, 'I was afraid you'd get so mad you'd go and kill him.'

'If he'd caught me I wouldn't have given up before I'd killed him.'

'Won't he come back now?'

'If he does I'll take care of him long before he gets here. Let's just see him take us away!'

'What if he has us shot?'

'Then I'll be dead, but I'll be of no use to him.'

'Nobody thinks of the life we have as being a life.'

'Only because we're so simple...'

In a little while their trough was filled with oilseed cake, hay, bran and grain, and the two friends began to eat. Jhuri stood by and stroked them while a couple of dozen boys watched the show.

Excitement seemed to have spread through the whole village.

At this moment the mistress of the house came out and kissed each of the bullocks on the forehead.

The Thakur's Well*

JOKHU BROUGHT THE *LOTA* TO HIS MOUTH BUT THE WATER smelled foul. He said to Gangi, 'What kind of water is this? It stinks so much I can't drink it! My throat's burning and you give me water that's turned bad.'

Every evening Gangi filled the water jugs. The well was a long way off and it was hard for her to make several trips. She'd brought this water yesterday and there'd been no bad smell at all. How could it be there now? She lifted the lota to her nostrils and it certainly smelt foul. Surely some animal must have fallen into the well and died. But she didn't know where else she could get any water.

No one would let her walk up to the Thakur's well. Even while she was far off, people would start yelling at her. At the other end of the village, the shopkeeper had a well but even there they wouldn't let her draw water. For people like herself there wasn't any well in the village.

Jhokhu, who'd been sick for several days, held back his thirst for a little while. Then he said, 'I'm so thirsty I can't stand it. Bring me the water, I'll hold my nose and drink a little.'

Gangi did not give it to him. His sickness would get worse from drinking bad water—that much she knew. But she didn't know that by boiling the water it would be made safe. She said, 'How

---

*Thakur Ka Kuan

can you drink it? Who knows what kind of beast has died in it?
I'll go and get you some water from the well.'

Surprised, Jokhu stared at her. 'Where can you get more water?'

'The Thakur and the shopkeeper both have wells. Won't they let me
fill just one lota?'

'You'll come back with your arms and legs broken, that's all. You'd
better just sit down and keep quiet. The Brahman will give a curse,
the Thakur will beat you with a stick, and that money-lending
shopkeeper takes five for every one he gives. Do you think people
like that are going to let you draw water from their wells.'

Harsh truth was in these words and Gangi could not deny it. But
she wouldn't let him drink that stinking water.

By nine at night the dead-tired field hands were fast asleep. Gangi
reached the Thakur's property to get water from his well.

The dim glow of a small oil lamp lit up the well. Gangi sat hidden
behind the wall and began to wait for the right moment. Everybody
in the village drank the water from his well. It was closed to
nobody; only those unlucky ones like herself could not fill their
buckets here.

Gangi [suddenly felt very angry.] Why was she so low and those
others so high? Because they wore a thread around their necks?
There wasn't one of them in the village who wasn't rotten. They
stole, they cheated, they lied in court, [then how were they so high
and mighty?]

She heard people approaching the well and her heart began to
pound. If anybody saw her, she'd get an awful kicking out of it. She
grabbed her bucket and rope and crept away to hide in the dark
shadows of a tree.

Two women had come to draw water and they were talking. One
said: 'There they were eating and they order *us* to get more water.'

'The men folk get jealous if they think they see us sitting around
taking it easy.'

'That's right, and you'll never see them pick up
the pitcher and fetch it themselves.
They just order us to get it as
though we were slaves.'

After they had filled their buckets
and left, Gangi came out from the
shadow of the tree and drew close
to the well platform. The idlers had
left, the Thakur had shut his door
and gone inside to the courtyard to
sleep. Gangi took a moment to sigh
with relief. On every side, the field was
clear. Gangi tiptoed up on to the well
platform. Never before had she felt
such a sense of triumph.

She looped the rope around the
bucket. Like some soldier stealing into
the enemy's fortress at night she peered
cautiously on every side. If she were
caught now, the slightest hope of
mercy or leniency won't be there.
Finally, with a prayer to the gods, she
mustered her courage and cast the
bucket into the well.

Slowly, slowly it sank in the water. There was not the slightest sound. Gangi yanked it back up with all her might to the rim of the well. No strong-armed athlete could have dragged it up more swiftly.

She had just stooped to catch it and set it on the wall when suddenly the Thakur's door opened. The jaws of a tiger could not have terrified her more.

The rope escaped from her hand. With a crash the bucket fell into the water, the rope after it, and for a few seconds there were sounds of splashing.

Yelling 'Who's there? Who's there?' the Thakur came toward the well and Gangi jumped from the platform and ran way as fast as she could.

When she reached home, Jokhu, with the lota at his mouth, was drinking that filthy, stinking water.

My Big Brother*

MY BIG BROTHER WAS FIVE YEARS OLDER THAN ME but only three grades ahead. He'd begun his studies at the same age I had but he didn't like the idea of moving hastily in an important matter like education. He wanted to lay a firm foundation for that great edifice, so he took two years to do one year's work; sometimes he even took three. If the foundations weren't well-made, how could the edifice endure?

I was nine, he was fourteen. He had full right by seniority to supervise and instruct me. And I was expected to accept every order of his as law.

By nature he was very studious. He was always sitting with a book open. And perhaps to rest his brain he would sometimes draw pictures of birds, dogs and cats in the margin of his notebook. Occasionally he would write a name, a word or a sentence ten or twenty times. He might copy a couplet out several times in beautiful letters or create new words which made no rhyme or reason.

I wasn't really very keen about studying. To pick up a book and sit with it for an hour was a tremendous effort. As soon as I found a chance I'd leave the hostel and go to the field and play marbles or fly paper kites or sometimes just meet a chum—what could be

---

*Bare Bhai Sahab

more fun? But as soon as I came back into the room and saw my brother's scowling face I was petrified. His first question would be, 'Where were you?' Always this question, always asked in the same tone and the only answer I had was silence. I don't know why I couldn't manage to say that I'd just been outside playing. My silence was an acknowledgement of guilt and my brother's only remedy for this was to greet me with indignant words.

'If you study English this way you'll be studying your whole life and you won't get one word right! Studying English is no laughing matter that anyone who wants to can learn. You've got to wear out your eyes morning and night and use every ounce of energy, then maybe you'll master the subject. And even then it's just to say you have a smattering of it. Even great scholars can't write proper English, to say nothing of being able to speak it. And I ask you, how much of a blockhead are you that you can't learn a lesson from looking at me? You've seen with your own eyes how much I grind. No matter how many shows and carnivals there may be have you ever seen me going to watch them? Every day there are cricket and hockey matches but I don't go near them. I keep on studying all the time, and even so it takes me two years or even three for one grade. So how do you expect to pass when you waste your time playing like this? Why waste our dad's hard-earned money?'

Hearing a dressing-down like this I'd start to cry. My brother was an expert in the art of giving advice. He'd say such sarcastic words, overwhelm me with such good counsel that my spirits would collapse, my courage disappear. I'd think, 'Why *don't* I run away from school and go back home? Why should I spoil my life fiddling with work that's beyond my capacity?' But after an hour or two the cloud of despair would clear away and I'd resolve to study with all my might. I'd draw up a schedule on the spot. How could I start work without first making an outline, working out a plan? In my timetable the heading of play was entirely absent. Get up at the crack of dawn, wash hands and face at six, eat a snack, sit down and study. From six to eight English, eight to nine arithmetic, nine to nine-thirty history, then meal-time and afterwards off to school. A half hour's rest at 3.30 when I got back from school, geography from four to five, grammar from five to six, then a half hour's walk in front of the hostel, six-thirty to seven English composition, then supper, translation from eight to nine, Hindi from nine to ten, from ten to eleven miscellaneous, then to bed.

But it's one thing to draw up a schedule, another to follow it. It began to be neglected from the very first day. The inviting green expanse of the playground, the balmy winds, the commotion on the football field, the exciting stratagems of prisoner's-base, the speed and flurries of volleyball would all draw me mysteriously and irresistibly. As soon as I was there I forgot everything: the life-destroying schedule, the

books that strained your eyes—I couldn't remember them at all. And then my big brother would have an occasion for sermons and scoldings. I would stay well out of his way, try to keep out of his sight, come into the room on tiptoe so he wouldn't know. But if he spotted me I'd just about die.

The yearly exams came round: my brother failed, I passed and was first in my class. Only two year's difference was left between him and me. Now I could be a little proud of myself and indeed my ego expanded. My brother's sway over me was over. I began to take part freely in the games, my spirits were running high. One day when I'd spent the whole morning playing stick-ball and came back exactly at meal-time, he said, with all the air of pulling out a sword to rush at me:

'I see you've passed this year and you're first in your class, and you've got stuck up about it. But my dear brother, even great men live to regret their pride, and who are you compared to them? You must have read about what happened to Ravan. Just to pass an exam isn't anything, the real thing is to develop your mind. Understand the significance of what you read. Ravan was master of the earth. Such kings are called 'Rulers of the World'. All the kings of the earth paid taxes to him. Great divinities were his slaves, even the gods of fire and water. But what happened to him in the end? Pride completely finished him off, destroying even his name. There wasn't anybody left to perform all his funeral rites properly. A man can commit any sin he wants but he'd better not be proud. When he turns proud he loses both this world and the next. You've just been promoted one grade and your head's turned by it.

'Don't assume that because I failed I'm stupid and you're smart. When you reach my class you'll sweat right through your teeth when you have to bite into algebra and geometry and study English history—it's not easy to memorize these king's names. There

were eight Henrys—do you think it's easy to remember all
the things that happened in each Henry's time? If you
write Henry the Eighth instead of Henry the
Seventh you get a zero. There were
dozens of Jameses, dozens of
Williams and scores of
Charleses! You get dizzy
with them, your mind's in a
whirl. Those poor fellows didn't
have names enough to go around. After
every name they have to put second, third,
fourth and fifth. If anybody'd asked me I could have reeled off
thousands of names. And as for geometry, well God help you! If you
write *a c b* instead of *a b c* your whole answer is marked wrong. If
you bring this perpendicular line down on that line it will be twice
the base line. I ask you, what's the point of that? If it isn't twice as
long it's four times as long or half as long, what do I care? But
you've got to pass so you've got to memorize all.

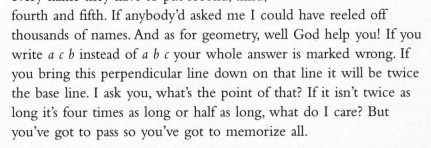

'They say, "Write an essay on punctuality no less than four pages long."
So now you open up your notebook in front of you, take your pen
and [hate] the whole business. Who doesn't know that punctuality's a
very good thing? A man's life is organized according to it, others love
him for it and his business prospers from it. How can you write four
pages on something so trifling? Do I need four pages for what I can
describe in one sentence? It's not economizing time, it's wasting it. We
want a man to say what he has to say quickly and then get moving.
It's a contradiction for them to ask us to write concisely. Write a
concise essay on punctuality in no less than four pages. All right! If
four pages is concise then maybe otherwise they'd ask us to write
one or two hundred pages. Run fast and walk slow at the same time.
Is that all mixed up or isn't it? When you get into my class, you'll really
take a beating, and then you'll find out what's what. Just because you
got a first division this time you're all puffed up—so pay attention
to what I say. What if I failed, I'm still older than you, I have more
experience of the world. Take what I say to heart or you'll be sorry.'

It was almost time for school, otherwise I don't know when this
medley of sermons would have ended. I didn't have much appetite

that day. If I got a scolding like this when I passed, maybe if I'd
failed I would have had to pay with my life. My brother's terrible
description of studying in the ninth grade really scared me. I'm
surprised I didn't run away from school and go home. But even a
scolding like this didn't change my distaste for books a bit, I didn't
miss one chance to play. I also studied, but much less. Well, anyway, just enough to complete the day's assignment and not be
disgraced in class. But the confidence I'd gained in myself
disappeared and then I began to lead a life like a thief's.

Then it was the yearly exams again and it so happened that once
more I passed and my brother failed again. I hadn't done much
work; but somehow or other I was in the first division. I myself was
astonished. My brother had just about killed himself with work,
memorizing every word in the course, studying till ten at night and
starting again at four in the morning, and from six until 9.30 before
going to school. He'd grown pale. But the poor fellow failed again
and I felt sorry for him. When he heard the results he broke down
and cried, and so did I. My pleasure in passing was cut by half.

There was only one grade left between my brother and me. The evil
thought crossed my mind that if he failed just once more I'd be at
the same level as him and then what grounds would he have for
lecturing me? But I violently rejected this unworthy idea. After all,
he'd scolded me only with the intention of helping me. At the time it
was really bad, but maybe it was only as a result of his advice that I'd
passed so easily and with such good marks.

Now my brother had become much gentler toward me. Several
times when he found occasion to scold me he did it without losing
his temper. Perhaps he himself was beginning to understand that he
no longer had the right to tell me off or at least not so much as
before. My independence grew. I began to take unfair advantage of his
toleration, I half started to imagine that I'd pass next time whether I
studied or not, my luck was high. As a result, the little I'd studied
before because of my brother, even that ceased. I found a new
pleasure in flying kites and now I spent all my time at the sport. Still,

I minded my manners with my brother and concealed my kite-flying from him. In preparation for the kite tournament I was secretly busy solving such problems as how best to secure the string and how to apply the paste mixed with ground glass in it to cut the other fellows' kites off their strings. I didn't want to let my brother suspect that my respect for him had in any way diminished.

One day, far from the hostel, I was running along like mad trying to grab hold of a kite. A whole army of boys came racing out to welcome it with long, thick bamboo rods. Nobody was aware who was in front or in back of him.

Suddenly I collided with my brother, who was probably coming back from the market. He grabbed my hand and said angrily, 'Aren't you ashamed to be running with these ragamuffins after a one-paisa kite? Have you forgotten that you're not in a low grade any more? You're in the eighth now, one behind me. A man's got to have some regard for his position, after all.

'I'm sorry to see you have so little sense. You're smart, there's no doubt of that, but what use is it if it destroys your self-respect? You must have assumed, "I'm just one grade behind my brother so now he doesn't have any right to say anything to me." But you're mistaken. I'm five years older than you and even if you come into my grade today that difference of five years between us not even God—to say nothing of you—can remove. I'm five years older than you and I always will be. The experience I have of life and the world you can never catch up with even if you get an M.A. and a D.Litt. and even a Ph.D. Understanding doesn't come from reading books. Our mother never passed any grade and Dad probably never went beyond the fifth, but even if we studied the wisdom of the whole world mother and father would always have the right to explain to us and to correct us. Not just because they're our parents but because they'll always have more experience of the world. Maybe they don't know what kind of government they've got in America or how many constellations there are in the sky, but there are a thousand things they know more about than you or me. God forbid, but if I should fall sick today then you'd be [at your wit's end]. You wouldn't be able to think of anything except sending a telegram to Dad. But in your place *he* wouldn't send anybody a telegram or get upset or be all flustered. First of all he'd diagnose the disease himself and try the remedy; then if it didn't work he'd call some doctor. But you and I don't even know how to make our allowance last through the month. We spend what father sends us and then we're penniless again. But as much as you and I spend today, Dad's maintained himself honourably and in good reputation the greater part of his life and brought up a family on half of it. So brother, don't be so proud of having almost caught up with me and being independent now. I'll see that you don't go off the track. If you don't mind, then (showing me his fist) I can use this too. I know you don't like hearing all this.'

I was thoroughly shamed by this new approach of his. I had truly come to know my own insignificance and a new respect for my brother was born in my heart. With tears in my eyes, I said, 'No, no, what you say is completely true and you have the right to say it.'

My brother embraced me and said, 'I don't forbid you to fly kites. I'd like to too. But what can I do? If I go off the track myself then how can I watch out for you? That's my responsibility.'

Just then by chance a kite that had been cut loose passed over us with its string dangling down. A crowd of boys were chasing after it. My brother is very tall and leaping up he caught hold of the string and ran at top speed toward the hostel and I ran close behind him.

The Naive Friends*

A BIRD HAD LAID EGGS JUST ABOVE THE CORNICE IN Keshav's house. Both Keshav and his sister, Shyama, would watch the bird intently, as it flew back and forth. First thing every morning, the two would come and stand in front of the cornice, rubbing their eyes, barely awake. The pleasure they drew from seeing the two birds was so great that they even forgot about the joys of milk and *jalebi*. Numerous questions rose in their minds: How big were the eggs? What colour were they? How many? What did they eat? How would the chicks come out of them? What is the nest like? But there was nobody around to answer their questions. Ma had no time from the housework and Babuji from his books. The two children had to comfort themselves by asking and answering each other.

Shyama: 'Tell me, Bhaiya, will the chicks fly away as soon as they come out of the eggs?'

'No, Silly,' Keshav would reply, proud as a scholar. 'First they have to grow wings. How would the poor things fly without wings?'

Shyama: 'What would the poor bird feed her little ones?' This was a tricky question for even Keshav to answer.

A couple of days went by and the children's curiosity increased. They were eager to see the eggs. They were certain they had hatched by

*Nadan Dost

then. The question of what the chicks would eat now weighed heavily on their minds. Where would the poor bird find enough grain to feed her brood? The chicks were sure to starve to death.

This thought left the siblings very anxious. They decided to scatter some grain on the cornice for the bird to pick. Shyama said happily, 'Oh! Then the bird won't have to fly anywhere in search of food, will she?'

'Oh no!' said Keshav. 'Why would she!'

'But won't the chicks be really hot up there?' a new worry crossed Shyama's mind.

Keshav had not thought of this problem until then. 'Yes!' he said. 'They are probably dying of thirst up there. There is no shade above them even.'

It was finally decided that a makeshift roof would be erected above the nest. The proposal for a bowl of water and some grain of rice was also approved.

Both children began to work in earnest. Shyama quietly brought some rice from the clay pot. Keshav secretly emptied the stone bowl of its oil, scrubbed it clean, and refilled it with water.

But where to get the cloth for the shelter? And how to make the roof stay up without support? Keshav puzzled over the problem for a while before it was finally resolved. 'Go and bring the garbage basket... make sure Ma doesn't see you.'

'But it's got a hole in the middle! Will it keep the sun out?'

'First, bring the basket,' Keshav said with slight irritation. 'I'll take care of the hole.' Shyama went running and returned with the basket. Keshav stuffed the hole with some paper and rested the basket against the branch of a nearby tree. 'See, how the shadow of the basket falls on the nest? The sun can't get through now!'

Shyama thought admiringly how clever her brother was.

It was the month of summer. Babuji had gone to work. Having put both children to sleep, Ma had lain down to rest. But the children were nowhere near sleeping. Eyes shut, they held their breath and waited for the right moment. As soon as they were sure Ma was asleep, they got up quietly, unlatched the door, and crept out. Soon they were making preparations to safeguard the eggs. Keshav brought a stool from the room, but it was still not high enough to reach the cornice. He then brought a small bathing stool to place under the first and gingerly climbed on top.

Shyama held the stool with both hands. Its uneven legs made it rather wobbly, and it tipped slightly, whichever way the pressure increased. Only Keshav knew what fear, what dread assailed him at that moment. He would grab the cornice to steady himself, and scold Shyama under his breath, 'Hold fast or I'll come down and beat you nicely.' But poor

Shyama's attention was taken up by the cornice. Time and again her mind veered in that direction, and her grip on the stool slackened.

The moment Keshav's hands reached the cornice, the birds flew away. Keshav saw some twigs scattered on the cornice, and three eggs lying on them. There was no nest like the ones he had seen on trees. Shyama asked, 'Can you see any chicks, Bhaiya?'

'There are three eggs; the chicks haven't come out yet.'

'Show me, Bhaiya! How big are they?'

'I will. But first bring some rags to lay under the eggs. The poor eggs are lying on twigs and straw.'

Shyama ran out and returned with a piece of cloth torn out from an old sari. Keshav leaned to take it from her, folded it a number of times to make it into a cushion and placed it under the eggs.

'I also want to see them, Bhaiya,' Shyama pleaded.

'Yes, yes. I will show them to you. But first bring the basket so that I can make a roof,' replied Keshav.

Shyama handed the basket from below and said, 'Now you come down, it's my turn.'

Keshav rested the basket against the branch and said, 'Go, bring the water and grain. Let me get down and then you can have a look.'

Shyama brought the bowl of water and rice too. Keshav placed them both under the basket and climbed down softly.

Shyama begged once again: 'Bhaiya, help me climb up too so I can see!'

'You'll fall down.'

'I won't fall down, Bhaiya! You hold the stool.'

'No, No, No, if you fall down, Ma will make chutney out of me. She will accuse me of helping you up. What will come out of your seeing them, anyway? Now the eggs are comfortable. When they hatch, we'll both look after the chicks.'

The two birds would approach the cornice only to quickly fly away again. Keshav wondered if they were scared and he took away the stools.

Shyama was tearful. 'You didn't show me,' she complained. 'I'll tell Ma.'

'I'll bash you if you tell Ma.'

'Then why didn't you show me?'

'And what if you had fallen down and broken your head?'

'So what? Big deal! You just wait, I'll tell Ma.' Just then the door opened and Ma came out, shielding her eyes from the blazing sun. 'What are you two doing out there in the sun?' she asked. 'Who opened the latch? How many times do I have to tell you not to come out in the afternoon?'

Keshav had opened the latch, but Shyama didn't say that to Ma. She was scared that he might get a beating. Keshav was afraid that Shyama might squeal. He hadn't shown her the eggs, and so didn't trust her. Whether Shyama was silent out of love or because she was party to the crime is a matter of some conjecture. Perhaps it was both.

Ma scolded them and took them both back inside the room. She latched the door and started fanning them softly. It was only two o'clock in the afternoon and the hot summer wind was blowing outside. Soon, the two children were sleeping soundly.

Shyama woke up with a start at four o'clock. The door was unlatched. She ran to the cornice, and looked up. There was no sign of the basket. She chanced to look down, ran back to the room and shouted, 'Bhaiya, the eggs have fallen down, the chicks have flown away.'

Keshav ran to the cornice and saw that the three eggs lay broken on the floor. A slimy white and yellow liquid was oozing out of them. The bowl of water was also lying upturned.

Keshav went pale and stared at the ground with gloomy eyes.

'Where have the chicks flown to?' Shyama asked.

'The eggs are broken,' Keshav said sadly.

'And where have the chicks gone?'

'Where do you think?' he replied with some irritation. 'Can't you see the white liquid coming out. It would have turned into chicks in a few days.'

Ma shouted from behind, 'What are you two doing out in the sun?'

'Ma! Ma! The eggs are broken,' said Shyama.

'You must have fiddled with them,' said Ma angrily, looking at the broken shells.

Now Shyama didn't pity her brother. He must not have put the eggs back carefully enough so that they had rolled off. He ought to be punished.

'He touched the eggs, Ma,' said Shyama.

'Why?' Ma asked.

Keshav stood tongue-tied.

'How did you reach there?' Ma asked again.

'He kept a stool on the bathing stool and climbed up,' Shyama said.

'Weren't you holding the stool?' Keshav charged.

'You told me to!' replied Shyama.

'You are a grown–up boy, Keshav,' said Ma. 'Don't you know that when you touch birds' eggs they become tainted, and then the birds don't hatch them anymore?'

'So the birds dropped the eggs themselves?' Shyama asked her mother fearfully.

'What else would the birds do!' Ma said. 'Keshav you have done a terrible thing. Oh my God! You have taken three lives.'

Keshav looked pained. 'I only cushioned the eggs,' he said quietly.

That made Ma laugh, but for quite some time after that Keshav was pricked by a guilty conscience. In trying to protect the eggs, he had destroyed them—this thought would even make him cry at times.

As for the two birds, they were never to be seen there again.

The Power of a Curse*

 IN THE VILLAGE OF CHANDPUR *MUNSHI* RAMSEVAK WAS A VERY rich man. He could be seen every day seated on a broken bench under a *neem* tree within the precincts of the open-air small-pleas court. Nobody had ever seen him presenting a brief before the tribunal or arguing a case; but everyone called him 'attorney'. Whenever he made his way to the open court the villagers crowded after him. He was regarded by everyone with respect and trust, and he was renowned for possessing the eloquence of the divine Saraswati herself. But it was only maintaining a family tradition. He had no very great income. His real means of livelihood was provided by widows without family and by old men with lots of money and little sense. The widows handed over their money to him for safe-keeping and old men who feared their worthless sons entrusted their wealth to him. But once any money went into his fist it forgot the way to come out again.

In the same village lived a Brahman widow named Munga. Her husband had been a sergeant in the native Indian battalion in Burma and had died in battle there. In view of his fine service, the government had bestowed a sum of rupees 500 on her. Being a

*Garib Ki Hay

widow and times being hard, the poor creature entrusted all her money to Ramsevak, and begging back tiny sums every month she managed to eke out a living.

Munshi*ji* had carried out his duty for several years now with full honesty. But when Munga had grown old without any sign of dying and he realized that perhaps from the whole amount she did not intend to leave even half to pay for her funeral expenses, he said to her one day, 'Munga, are you going to die or aren't you? Or just say straight out that you'll look after your own funeral fees.' That day Munga's eyes were opened, and she said, 'Give me back the full amount!' The account book was ready: not a pice of it remained according to the book. She violently grabbed his hand and said, 'You've taken 250 rupees of mine but I won't let you keep a pice of it!'

But a poor widow's anger has little effect. She didn't have any influence in the courts, she couldn't read or write or keep accounts. To be sure, there was some hope in the *panchayat*, the village council. The panchayat met, people gathered from several villages. Munshi Ramsevak was ready and agreeable; he stood up in the council and addressed the members: 'Friends! You are all noble and devoted to the truth. I bow to you all. I am grateful to the core to you for your generosity and mercy, your charity and love. Do you people think I really took the money of this unfortunate widow?'

With one voice the councillors said, 'No, no! You couldn't do such a thing!'

Munshiji said, 'If you all agree that I've stolen her money, then there'll be nothing left for me except to drown myself. I'm not a rich man, nor can I take pride in being munificent. But thanks to my pen and to your kindness I cannot call myself needy. Am I so petty as to steal a widow's money?'

The councillors were unanimous. 'No, no, you couldn't do such a thing!'

The council acquitted him.

Munga heaved a sigh and, making the most of it, said to herself, 'If I'm not to get it here, then all right, I won't, but I'll get it back in heaven.'

There was nobody now to help Munga or listen to her grieving. Whatever woes poverty bestowed she had to bear them all. She was strong of body and if she had wanted she could have worked hard. But from the day the panchayat gave its judgment she swore she wouldn't work. Now she was obsessed with the thought of her money. All day and all night, walking or sitting, she had only one idea: to inveigh against Munshi Ramsevak.

Gradually her mind gave way. Bare-headed, bare-bodied, with a little hatchet in her hand, she would sit in desolate places. She abandoned her hut and was seen wandering around the ruins in a cremation *ghat* along the river—dishevelled, red-eyed, grimacing crazily, her arms and legs emaciated. When they saw her like this people were frightened. Now no one teased her even for fun. Whenever she came out in the village, women shut the doors of their houses, men slunk away and children ran off screeching. But there was one child who didn't run away and that was Munshiji's son Ramgulam. The village one-eyed and lame men hated the sight of him. He would keep after Munga, clapping his hands and taking the village dogs with him, until the poor woman, utterly bewildered, would flee the hamlet. Having lost her mind along with her money she had earned the title of the local mad-woman. She would sit alone, talking to herself for hours, expressing her intense desire to harm Ramsevak, and when her hatred reached its climax she would turn her face toward Ramsevak's house and shriek the terrible words, 'I'll drink your blood!'

Munshiji was a man of great courage and tenacity, but when he heard Munga's awful words he was scared. We may not be afraid of human justice but the fear of God's justice resides in every man's heart—Munga's dreadful night-wanderings sometimes inspired such reflections in Ramsevak's mind, and even more in his wife's.

Nagin was a very shrewd woman. She advised her husband about all his business dealings. She was as brilliant in speech as he in writing.

One midnight when Munshiji had gone to sleep, suddenly Munga let out a shriek right on his doorstep and howled, 'I'll drink your blood!'

Munshiji was electrified by her horrible peals of laughter. His legs shook with fear, his heart thumped. Gathering up his courage with a great effort he opened the door and woke Nagin.

The two of them tiptoed to the threshold and peeking from the door they saw Munga's dim figure lying on the ground, they heard her panting.

The night passed. The door was shut but Ramsevak and Nagin spent the hours sitting up. Munga could not get inside but who could stop her voice? Her voice was the most terrible thing about her.

The news got around the village that Munga was squatting on Munshiji's doorstep. The villagers took great delight in his embarrassment and loss of face. Whole flocks of people gathered around at once. Little Ramgulam didn't like this crowd and he got so angry with Munga that if he had had the power he would have flung her into a well. Ramgulam collected the dung of their cow in a pot and flung it at

the poor woman. Some of it splashed on the onlookers too. Munga was completely covered and the people hastily retreated, saying, 'This is Munshi Ramgulam's door where you can expect such fine manners!' Munshiji congratulated his son on this ingenious and appealing way of getting rid of that good-for-nothing crowd. The whole mob finally disappeared, but Munga went on lying there exactly as before.

That night Munga neither ate nor drank anything and once again Munshiji and Nagin lay awake until morning. By now Munga's howling and laughing were heard much less frequently. The people of the household assumed that the worst was over. As soon as it was daylight Munshiji opened the door and saw Munga lying motionless.

It is impossible to describe the sensation this event produced in the village and the extent of Ramsevak's disgrace. Whatever prestige he'd been able to maintain vanished. Munga had come to die on his doorstep. She knew she could not accomplish much alive but dead she could do a great deal.

Munshi Ramsevak was versed in law: according to the law he was innocent. Munga had not died according to any legal instance, no example of it could be found in the Indian Penal Code. Throughout the day Munshiji and his wife consoled themselves with such reasoning. But as soon as it was evening their rationalizing petered out.

Fear took hold of them when darkness fell. As the hour turned late this fear grew all the stronger. They'd left the front door open by mistake and not one of them was daring enough to get up and shut it. Finally Nagin took a lamp, Munshiji his axe and Ramgulam the sickle, and the three of them, quaking and shrinking, went to the door. After closing the door, the three of them went into the kitchen and began to cook something.

But Munga had got under their skins. Seeing their own shadow they'd jump, sure it was Munga. It seemed to them that she was sitting in every dark corner.

In the kitchen they had set several large clay pots for flour and pulse and there were some old rags lying around too. Driven by hunger a mouse came out looking for the grain.

The mouse crept under the rags with a rustling sound. The way those rags were spread out they looked exactly like Munga's skinny legs. When she saw them Nagin jumped and let

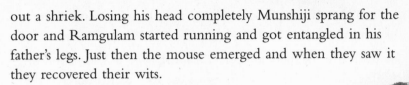

out a shriek. Losing his head completely Munshiji sprang for the door and Ramgulam started running and got entangled in his father's legs. Just then the mouse emerged and when they saw it they recovered their wits.

After they'd eaten the three of them came into the bedroom. But even there Munga did not leave them alone. They were talking, enjoying themselves. But even in these diversions Munga's image refused to leave their minds. The very slightest tap would startle them. If there was a rustling of leaves the hair would stand up on all three of them.

At midnight Nagin was startled from her sleep. It seemed to her that Munga, with her red eyes and sharp pointed teeth, was sitting on her chest. Nagin screamed. She started running toward the courtyard like a madwoman, and suddenly she fell senseless to the ground, sweating all over. Munshiji had been awakened by her yell but he was so frightened he didn't open his eyes. Like a blind man he felt his way to the door. After a long while he found it and came into the courtyard. Nagin was lying on the ground. Fear of Munga had killed her. While Munga lived she had always feared Nagin's hissing. But sacrificing her own life, she could now take Nagin's.

Having done away with Nagin, Munga was not going to leave Munshiji alone. At every moment her image remained before his eyes. Wherever he might be his mind always harked back to her.

Like a prisoner in solitary confinement, somehow or other he managed to get through the next ten or twelve days. At the end of two weeks, his mourning over, Munshiji changed his clothes and with his mat and satchel went to the open court. Today his expression was a little brighter. Today, he thought, his clients would flock around him, they'd condole with him and he'd shed a few tears. Then there would be an abundance of foreclosures, settlements and mortgages and he'd be rolling in money. Full of these thoughts he reached the court.

But there, instead of the abundance of mortgages and the flood of foreclosures and the merry greetings of clients, he encountered the sandy wastes of disappointment. He sat for hours with his satchel open but nobody came near him, or even inquired about how he was. Not only were there no new clients but very old ones, whose business Munshiji's family had handled for generations, today hid their faces from him. After wasting his whole day at the court Munshiji went home, sunk in worry and disappointment. As soon as he came close to the house Munga's image rose before him. He was so nervous that when on opening the door two dogs, shut in by Ramgulam, came rushing out he completely lost his wits, let out a shriek and fell senseless to the ground.

What happened to Munshiji after this is not known. For several days people saw him go to the court and come back drooping. After that he went off to the shrine of Badrinath and was not seen for several months.

One day a sadhu came to the village—on his forehead ashes, locks long and matted, a clay waterpot in his hand. His countenance closely resembled Ramsevak's and his speech also was not much different. He sat in meditation beneath a tree. That night smoke rose from Ramsevak's house, the glow of a fire was visible and then a burst of flame.

As for Ramgulam, when Munshiji disappeared he went off to live with an uncle and stayed there a while, but no one there could put up with his ways.

One day he was digging up radishes in somebody's field. The owner gave him a few slaps. This made him so angry that he went into the man's granary and set it on fire. It burned down completely and thousands of rupees went up in smoke. The police investigated and Ramgulam was arrested. For this offence he is at present in the reformatory at Chunar.

Glossary

anna:	unit of currency (now obsolete); one-sixteenth of a rupee
baba:	exclamation meaning giving up in disgust; also signifies a holy person
bhang:	a narcotic preparation, sometimes mixed with food or drink
bhaiya:	brother
bigha:	a measure of land
Brahman:	the priestly caste
chapatti:	thin, soft, round, unleavened baked wheat bread; same as roti
Chaudhri:	leader, usually the headman in a village
dharma:	depending on context, dharma means religion, duty, morality, moral principles, obligation, righteousness
dhoti:	a long piece of cloth that is wrapped around the lower half of the body; traditional lower garment for men
ekka:	small carriage drawn by a single horse
ghee:	clarified butter
Gond:	indicates a person of a very low-ranking social group, especially in eastern Uttar Pradesh
gulab-jamun:	a type of sweet
halva:	soft sweet made with ghee, sugar, or syrup, and spices combined with carrots or some other basic ingredient
hookah:	a water pipe for smoking tobacco
Huzoor:	old-fashioned term of address for a person of high social standing
jalebi:	a type of sweet
khus:	fragrant root of a grass used for cooling purposes
leechee:	a bright red stone fruit with a white fleshy edible aril

lota:	small round pot, usually made of copper or brass for water or other drinkable fluids
Maharaj:	literally great king or conqueror; often used as term of address to a Brahman or to a superior
mahatma:	literally 'great soul'; a saint or saintly person; also used ironically
maund:	a measure of weight, equal to *c.* 40 kg
memsahib:	used formerly in colonial India as a form of respectful address for a European woman; also a humorous or ironic way of referring to a westernized woman; a woman sahib
Munshi:	title of respect for an educated man
paan:	betel leaf folded over lime, tobacco, and spices; usually taken after a meal
panchayat:	council of elders that governs the village
Pandit:	learned man, often of the Brahman caste
pice:	variant spelling of paisa (unit of currency); one-hundredth of a rupee
puri:	round, soft, unleavened, deep-fried wheat bread; regarded as more special than a chapatti
Ram Ram:	the repeated name of Rama, hero of the Ramayana, used as greeting among Hindus
sahib:	a polite form of address, often placed after a person's name or title; a gentleman
Savan:	fifth month of the Hindu calendar corresponding to July–August; monsoon season in north India
Shastri, -ji:	versed in the *shastras* (religious scriptures)
Thakur:	man of high caste, a Brahmin; often a ruling class

Note on Translators

DAVID RUBIN has spent many years teaching Indian literature at Columbia University and Sarah Lawrence College. A widely-published writer, his works of fiction include *The Great Darkness* (1963) which won the British Author's Club Award for best first novel in 1963. Among his translation works are *Nirmala* (1988), *The Return of Sarasvati: Four Hindi Poets* (OUP, 1998), *Widows, Wives and Other Heroines* (OUP, 1998), and *The World of Premchand: Selected Short Stories* (OUP, 2001).

KHUSHWANT SINGH is a renowned journalist and the author of several works of fiction. A former editor of the *Illustrated Weekly of India*, and the *Hindustan Times*, he was Member of Parliament from 1980 to 1986. He has authored a number of translations, and is considered an authority on Sikh religion, culture, and history.

PRIYANKA SARKAR is a postgraduate student of English Literature at the University of Delhi.

Note on Illustrator

MANJARI CHAKRAVARTI is an award-winning artist from Shantiniketan, with a special interest in illustration, particularly for children's books. Her work has travelled, via numerous solo and group exhibitions, both across the country and abroad.